"Just help me with a k

Wyatt's lips hovered above hers. Then, in true Buckhorn style, Wyatt claimed what he wanted. And then he wasn't just kissing her, but transporting her to another world.

A place where she wasn't alone and trying to hide that she was five months pregnant. When he finally released her, it was a struggle for Natalie to keep her rubbery knees from buckling.

"Damn..." Wyatt looked a little dazed himself. "Um, that went better than expected."

Natalie managed a nod.

"We good?"

"Ah, in what sense?" she asked.

"You know, like we're still pals?"

Pals? She choked back a laugh. If this was how he kissed a woman he thought of as his pal, she couldn't fathom what he'd do to an actual lover. "Um, sure."

"Thanks." After landing a sucker punch to Natalie's right shoulder, he nodded toward his scowling blonde date. "Pretty sure that did the trick."

Dear Reader,

Wyatt and Natalie's story marks the end of marriage-eligible Buckhorns! This makes me sad, but on the flip side, when I'm old and all the Buckhorn babies are grown, I suppose the saga can start over with all the new adult singles. For those of you who've read the whole series, can you even imagine what terrors Bonnie and Betsy will be while dating?

Looking back, it's interesting to see how as my fictional family has changed, my own has followed suit. In the year it's taken to write the four stories, my children have graduated from high school and gone on to college. I've gone from being an emotional train wreck over them leaving to now being buried under the pile of stuff they brought back home for summer! It's taking some adjusting, getting back in the habit of grabbing all of their favorites from the grocery store, but I think I'll manage just fine, as happy as I am to have them all snug in my nest.

In this last Buckhorn installment, Mama Buckhorn takes some grief from her offspring. They're put out with her for always having an opinion. But as a fellow mom, I say they should just behave and do what their mother tells them. Ha! Fat chance. Wyatt and Natalie have proven to be my most stubborn couple yet!

Happy reading,

Laura Marie

A Baby in His Stocking

LAURA MARIE ALTOM

TORONTO NEW YORK LONDON
AMSTERDAM PARIS SYDNEY HAMBURG
STOCKHOLM ATHENS TOKYO MILAN MADRID
PRAGUE WARSAW BUDAPEST AUCKLAND

Recycling progr
for this product
not exist in your area.

ISBN-13: 978-0-373-75387-1

A BABY IN HIS STOCKING

ABOUT THE AUTHOR

After college (Go, Hogs!), bestselling, award-winning author Laura Marie Altom did a brief stint as an interior designer before becoming a stay-at-home mom to boy-girl twins and a bonus son. Always an avid romance reader, she knew it was time to try her hand at writing when she found herself replotting the afternoon soaps.

When not immersed in her next story, Laura teaches art at a local middle school. In her free time, she beats her kids at video games, tackles Mount Laundry and of course reads romance!

Laura loves hearing from readers at either P.O. Box 2074, Tulsa, OK 74101, or by email, BaliPalm@aol.com.

Love winning fun stuff? Check out
www.lauramariealtom.com.

Books by Laura Marie Altom

HARLEQUIN AMERICAN ROMANCE
1028—BABIES AND BADGES
1043—SANTA BABY
1074—TEMPORARY DAD
1086—SAVING JOE*
1099—MARRYING THE MARSHAL*
1110—HIS BABY BONUS*
1123—TO CATCH A HUSBAND*
1132—DADDY DAYCARE
1147—HER MILITARY MAN
1160—THE RIGHT TWIN
1165—SUMMER LOVIN'
    "A Baby on the Way"
1178—DANCING WITH DALTON
1211—THREE BOYS AND A BABY
1233—A DADDY FOR CHRISTMAS
1257—THE MARINE'S BABIES
1276—A WEDDING FOR BABY**
1299—THE BABY BATTLE**
1305—THE BABY TWINS**
1336—THE BULL RIDER'S CHRISTMAS BABY***
1342—THE RANCHER'S TWIN TROUBLES***
1359—A COWGIRL'S SECRET***

*U.S. Marshals
**Baby Boom
***The Buckhorn Ranch

For eighteen-year-old dachshund Noodle Alisch.
You were a good dog and we loved you.
Hope you're off chasing a tennis ball
on a never-ending beach!

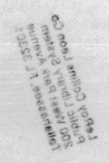

Chapter One

If Natalie Lewis felt any more emotionally battered, she'd dissolve into a teary puddle right there in the middle of Georgina Buckhorn's garden. Pregnant. Abandoned. Surrounded by dozens of happy, October-sun-drenched guests whose very presence dictated she force a smile. Around these parts, the christening of Josie and Dallas Buckhorn's new baby was huge. But how was she supposed to get into a celebratory frame of mind when hours earlier Craig had shattered her world?

She'd loved him and had assumed they'd be married and raise a family together. But then, silly her, she'd only been waiting for that ring on her finger for three years. What was wrong with her that she'd ignored every sign that Craig avoided commitment the way some folks steered clear of root canals? From not wanting to even hold hands in public to bailing on too many important occasions to count, Craig made a habit of reminding her just how little she meant in the overall scheme of his life. He even refused to sleep over on the Friday nights they made love. Oh, he'd invented his own art form when it came to stringing her along. Promising to spend more time with her when his work slowed. Explaining he'd just bought a calendar to help remember their dates. Ha! Fat lot of good that'd had done when he'd left it in a junk drawer. And he worked for UPS! Did they ever *slow down?* God, she was such an idiot.

"I need a favor."

Natalie glanced up to see Wyatt Buckhorn standing before her in all his glory. "I'm busy."

"Could've fooled me." He pried her cookie-filled plate from her hands, setting it on the table alongside her wicker love seat.

"Hey," she protested. "If ever there was a girl in need of cookie-therapy, it's me."

He rolled his eyes. "Cry me a river. Craig's been an ass before, and I'm sure he will again. This is important." Drawing her to her feet, he tugged her against him—tightly enough together a playing card couldn't have been slid between them. Though Natalie and Wyatt had been pals since their first day in Weed Gulch Elementary's kindergarten class, she couldn't ever remember touching him—not like this. He was a Buckhorn, and had everything that came with the name. Criminally handsome, filthy rich, with enough charisma to charm a rattler into being a lap pet. That said, she'd always viewed him as someone to study from afar. He moved in vastly different circles than she did, which was fine. Back in high school he dated only cheerleaders and she'd had no wish to break her arm in a cheerleading pyramid, or, now that they'd grown, his usual date's stiletto heels.

"Yeah," she snatched a cookie from her plate, "so is my strict comfort-food regime."

Fingers around her wrist, he playfully growled before biting off a good three-quarters of her treat.

Before she'd worked up a protest speech, he finished it off.

"Back to business," he said upon swallowing. "In about thirty seconds, I'm going to kiss you. If you play along, I'll forever be in your debt." With a tip of his cowboy hat, he looked as matter-of-fact as if he'd asked directions to the nearest bar.

Natalie lurched back far enough for the pool deck's wrought-iron fence to bite into her lower vertebrae. "How much champagne punch have you had?"

"Promise," he said in his lazy cowboy drawl, "I'm stone-cold sober. Plus, this whole godparent thing makes us practically family, and besides my date you're the only single female under the age of eighty and over the age of seven. You're my only hope."

"No," she insisted. "I've had the worst twenty-four hours in world history and—"

Leaning into her personal space, his warm, sugar-laced breath acted like a brick thrown against her resolve. In the lifetime they'd been casual friends, she couldn't recall Wyatt having ever stood so close. Her pulse behaved badly, galloping over her common sense at an alarming speed.

Licking suddenly parched lips, she managed to mutter, "So, yeah, it's been a lousy day for me and I probably should just go home."

"Hell." He inched still closer. "That's what you want, I'll drive you. Just first help me with a kiss."

Where Natalie's words used to live now resided hitched breath and the kind of tingly awareness she shouldn't be feeling. But this was Wyatt Buckhorn standing before her, begging for a kiss. The scene didn't make sense—not in her carefully ordered world.

"So we're good?" Wyatt asked, hovering his lips above hers.

No! This assault against her senses was miles from good. But then, in true Buckhorn style, Wyatt claimed what he wanted, pressing his lips to hers. And then he wasn't just kissing her, but transporting her to another world. A place where she wasn't alone and trying to hide that she was five months pregnant, but shimmering with a slow, honeyed warmth spreading from her head to her toes. Wyatt's kiss was firm yet gentle. Sinful and wicked, but in a heavenly realm of good.

When she moaned, he stole the opportunity to sweep her tongue with his. The broad, leisurely stroke was too much, drowning her in powerful, sexy heat. Arms on autopilot, they twined about his neck, and she pressed her fingertips to the back of his head, urging him in for still more. When he finally released her, it was a struggle for Natalie to keep her rubbery knees from buckling.

"Damn…" To Natalie's credit, Wyatt looked a little dazed himself by the power of what they'd shared. Did that mean it hadn't all been her imagination? "Um, that went better than expected."

Breathing still shallow, Natalie managed a nod.

He glanced away, red-faced. "We good?"

"Ah, in what sense?" she asked, doing a quick check to make sure her clothes hadn't spontaneously combusted from her superheated limbs.

"You know, like we're still pals?"

Pals? She choked back a laugh. If this was how he kissed a woman he thought of as his pal, she couldn't fathom the carnal gifts he'd dole out to an actual lover. "Um, sure."

"Thanks." After landing a sucker punch to Natalie's

right shoulder, he nodded toward his scowling date. "Pretty sure that did the trick."

"Everyone line up for more pictures!" Georgina Buckhorn, Wyatt's mother, was in her element. Parties were her thing, and the over-the-top angel-themed christening for Josie and Dallas's second daughter together, Esther, was no exception. A trio of harpists provided ethereal song to the gorgeous Indian-summer afternoon. Buffet tables dripping in vintage lace and pearls held outrageously opulent cakes, candies and tarts. Antique-pink roses perfumed the air. "Natalie and Wyatt, you two hold the baby alongside the fountain. Dallas, throw glitter at them so they sparkle."

"I'm not pitching glitter at my child," Dallas barked, handing Esther to his brother. As the eldest of the Buckhorn men, he was also the least playful. A fact that, at the moment, served Natalie well.

"Again," Wyatt whispered above the fountain's gurgle for only her to hear, "I appreciate you helping me out with that kiss. I've been hinting to Starla for days that I'm not the kind of guy who's in it for the long haul, but she refuses to listen. By helping me provide a few more visual clues, you made the perfect assist."

"Sure. No biggee." *Liar,* her conscience screamed. Part of her wanted to rail at him for including her in such a stupid stunt. Then there was the portion of Natalie still humming with awareness and craving more of whatever Wyatt cared to offer—and that girl wanted to thank him.

Georgina, camera in hand, directed, "I need a few with just the godparents. Natalie, you hold Esther. Wyatt, put your arm around Nat—and for heaven's sake, smile."

Unbearable didn't come close to describing the next

five minutes. As much as Natalie had always viewed Wyatt as a fixture in her life, like a brother, she had to admit—if only to herself—he'd grown into one of the most handsome men she'd ever seen. Tall and lanky with spiky black hair and impenetrable brown eyes, he was the dark horse to his fair-haired brothers and sister. He'd been the epitome of Weed Gulch High cool. Star quarterback for football. Pitcher for baseball. He'd changed girlfriends as often as clothes. *Wiley Wyatt,* he'd been nicknamed for his refusal to commit.

"Nat," Josie Buckhorn called, "scoot closer to Wyatt. He's not going to bite." Natalie's best friend, a petite redhead with freckles and a perpetual smile ever since marrying Dallas, gestured for Natalie to sidle up to Wyatt.

"I might. Bite, that is." He aimed a wink toward his already miffed blonde date, which sent her stomping toward the open bar.

Natalie sighed. Wyatt's action was perfect. Just the sort of thing needed to plant her feet solidly back on the ground. Their kiss might've been scorching, but it was also make-believe. And from a guy apparently every bit as commitment-phobic as Craig.

"Just a few more," Georgina said, adjusting Esther's bonnet, "and we ought to have enough."

The baby started to fuss.

"You're done," Dallas growled at his mom and the high-priced Tulsa photographer. Taking the baby into his arms, he too headed for the bar.

Josie chased after him carrying their other daughter, Mabel.

Leaving Natalie on her own with her *pal.*

He cleared his throat, extending his hand for her to

shake. "I really did appreciate your help. Sorry if our kiss got a little too, well…nice."

"Apology accepted." *Nice* wasn't the word she'd have chosen for the hot tingles still coursing through her body from his touch. Now she wholeheartedly understood why women flocked to him. She'd just never counted herself as being among his groupies.

The afternoon wore on and on and on.

Around three, Natalie searched out Josie to say her goodbyes.

Unfortunately, her best friend wasn't going to let her run out that easily. "Don't even think about getting out of here before spilling every detail of that kiss."

Josie held Esther. Judging by the baby's fitful cries, the one-month-old didn't realize that the party in full swing was in her honor. "Does this mean you and Wyatt have finally succumbed to your base urges to make out and then get married?" As usual, Josie made zero attempt to hide her desire for Natalie to hook up with Wyatt. She'd launched her campaign nearly two years earlier, when she'd married Dallas, and had yet to see the futility of her actions.

"Give it up," Natalie said with a heartfelt sigh. "I know you mean well, but trust me, this bizarre dream of yours will never come true."

"Then why'd you kiss him?" Josie winked.

"He kissed me. A sad tactic to unload his date just in time for all-night poker." While most guests still mingled around the pool and Georgina Buckhorn's renowned garden, Wyatt and his posse—the same guys he'd hung out with through high school and college—could be seen through the den's picture window setting up for the game. They played during or after most of

Georgina's parties; just because this was a christening made no difference to their routine.

"Still," Josie said, "it looked hot. Was it?"

Lie! Natalie's voice of reason screamed. If she showed the smallest chink in her Anti-Wyatt Wall, Josie would use it to her advantage. Shrugging, Natalie said, "I've had better."

Josie rolled her eyes. "Mark my words, one of these days you two will discover each other, and when you do—*pow!*" In the process of waving her arm, she startled the baby into a full-blown wail. "Oops. Shh…" Jiggle, jiggle. "Sorry, sweetie. Mommy didn't mean to scare you. She was just trying to make Auntie Nat see how much she secretly adores Uncle Wyatt."

"On that note…" Natalie kissed the crown of Esther's downy head. "I'm exhausted, but still have a few baskets to make for school tomorrow."

"Excuses, excuses." Josie's expression said she wasn't buying Natalie's exit speech. "See you in the morning."

"Looking forward to it— Oh, and if you get a sec after the festivities, would you mind rounding up any clothes Betsy and Bonnie have outgrown? I've got a few families in desperate need."

"Absolutely," Josie said, ambushing Natalie in a hug. "Thanks again for coming—and agreeing to be this one's godmother. It means the world to Dallas and me."

Natalie was Weed Gulch Elementary's counselor, where Josie taught kindergarten. Though it wasn't in her official job description, Natalie made care baskets she delivered anonymously to community families. Usually, she looked forward to organizing donated goods into utilitarian gifts, but as she climbed into her white VW bug all she truly wanted to do—aside from reliving Wyatt's criminally hot kiss—was take a nice, long nap.

"SINCE WHEN ARE YOU macking on Fatty Natty?"

Wyatt lowered his cards, giving his old pal Owen Fletcher a glare. "Lay off. Since Dallas married Josie, Nat's practically family, and I'd appreciate you treating her as such."

"Touchy," Owen said, getting up from the table for another beer. "This something we should know about?"

"Yeah," West Graham piped in, "what happened to the blonde you had hanging all over you less than an hour ago?"

Wyatt shrugged. "Starla was starting to get too serious."

Owen, a hulking former Weed Gulch and then University of Oklahoma offensive lineman, opened his beer. "Yeah, but you could have had a lot of fun with her on the way to full-on serious."

"Well, I didn't feel like having fun with her anymore," Wyatt grumbled. "Are we here to play or what?"

Owen's eyes widened. "All right, man. Jeez, what's wrong with a little fun, is all I'm saying."

"I don't know." In truth, Wyatt did know, but he wasn't about to spill the secret he hadn't even shared with his brothers. He tossed chips into the center pot. "I'm in and raise you five."

West, one of Weed Gulch's finest fullbacks, tossed in his chips, as well. "Sounds like someone's trying to change the subject."

"Not at all."

Owen added his chips to the pot.

"I'm just tired of chit-chat when I need to focus on

taking you two for all you're worth." Not to mention getting his mind off Natalie's kiss.

IN HER TEDDY-BEAR-THEMED office Monday morning, Natalie nursed a Sprite while making notes for the school's upcoming fifth-grade assembly on setting future goals. Before losing the kids to middle school, she drummed into them the importance of choosing a path and then following it. Ironic, in light of the mess she'd managed to make of her own life.

She nibbled a saltine, wishing the computer screen would quit swaying with each rush of nausea. How did she get the memo to her body that morning sickness was supposed to be gone by her second trimester?

Realizing she wasn't going to make it through reading the next sentence, Natalie dashed for the bathroom. She'd just rocked back to sit on her heels when Cami Vettle, the school secretary, pushed open the door.

"You ever going to admit you don't have a perpetual flu?"

Managing a sad laugh, Natalie said, "Is it that obvious?"

"To me. But then I spend five mornings a week with you. Who's the daddy?"

"If I had an ounce of energy—" Natalie rested her head against the cool, tile wall "—I'd jump up from here to smack you."

"I figured it was that gorgeous UPS guy," Cami said while passing a paper towel beneath cold water, "but you never know."

"Seriously?" Natalie groaned in pleasure when Cami placed the towel on her forehead. "You, of all people, know Craig's the only guy I've been with for the past three years."

After helping Natalie to her feet, Cami said, "When are you getting married?"

"We're not. The day after I told him our blessed news, he applied for a transfer. I never thought he'd really go, but *voilà*, five months in and baby's daddy up and moved to Miami."

"Oh, no."

Returning to her office, Natalie stretched out on her sofa.

Cami ruined Natalie's temporary peace by asking, "What are you going to do?"

In the months she'd had to ponder her situation, Natalie had given that particular question a lot of thought. She'd always wanted to be a mom. Sure, in her little-girl fantasies she'd been happily married when giving birth, but that didn't change the fact that, as much as Craig wanted nothing to do with their child, she looked forward to holding her baby in her arms. "I'll do the only thing I can—raise my child on my own."

"What do your parents think?"

Nausea struck again. "It's my fervent prayer they're not as observant as you."

THAT AFTERNOON, NATALIE felt much better. She'd managed to eat a little lunch and now stood in the empty auditorium, facing the twenty baskets lining the edge of the stage. She'd already rolled clothes, tying them with ribbon. Now she needed to add food, gift certificates from local merchants, books and toys.

The task she usually enjoyed felt daunting. One thing she hadn't expected with pregnancy was to be so tired. Not just the kind of slump fended off with coffee, but a deep-down exhaustion that clung to her shoulders, weighing her down. Moodiness was another symptom she hadn't expected. Everything from a dead fly to a Hallmark commercial made her cry.

She'd never been a fan of formfitting clothes, so hiding her condition for so long had been easier than she'd thought. That said, much more moodiness and it'd be her hormones giving her away rather than her baby bump.

"Hey," Josie's voice echoed through the lofty space. "Cami said I'd find you in here."

"Are your kids in art?"

"Yep. I should be grading, but yesterday's sugar has me feeling hungover."

"I know the feeling."

Familiar with the basket drill, Josie stepped up to help. Tucking canned chili between pint-size blue jeans and a puzzle, she said, "Cami told me you were sick again this morning. Also that you let her in on your secret. What prompted you to finally share your news?"

"I didn't. Turns out she'd guessed a long time ago. Anyway, it's not like I can keep my baby a secret much longer."

Josie attacked Natalie with a hug. Then she grabbed some more cans of food. "Have you been feeling any better?"

"No. I'm tired, cranky and my body refuses to choose between ravenous or nauseous."

From down the hall in the choir room came muted singing.

Natalie pressed her palms to her suddenly throbbing head.

"Honey," Josie asked, setting her cans on the stage floor, "what's wrong?"

Tears sprang hot and messy from nowhere. For

weeks, Natalie had tried controlling her panic, but something about holding sweet Esther and that surprise dreamy kiss with Wyatt and then getting sick had her hormones about as stable as a four-wheeler on a pot-holed dirt road. "I—I thought I could be strong—you know, raising this baby on my own, but I'm scared."

"Everything's going to be okay." Being wrapped in another of Josie's warm hugs should've made Natalie feel better, but if anything, her friend's kindness only served as a reminder to how easily she'd given her heart to Craig only to have him crush it like a recy-clable aluminum can. "Sweetie, you know I'll be here for you every step of the way. Heck, our house is big enough to hold half the county. If you have this baby and feel overwhelmed, move in with us and we'll all help out."

Her friend's offer brought on fresh tears. "Why couldn't Craig have been as perfect as you?"

Josie laughed through her own tears. "Wish I knew. I'd offer to drag him back and knock sense into him, but one of these days, if and when you're ready, you can do much better in the man and baby-daddy depart-ment. I want you to find someone as dreamy as Dallas. Not just for emotional support, but the little things like helping with late-night feedings and deciphering all those mysterious burps and coos."

Sighing, Natalie broke Josie's hold to pace the center aisle. "I'm happy for you and Dallas—really, I am—but as much as I thought you two were made for each other, that's how much I know I'm done with men. Before Craig, there was Neil. Remember him? The guy who took two dates to the same party? And who could forget Sam? The one who dumped me for a woman

Chapter Two

"Sure this is what you want to do?"

Wyatt signed off on the last of the paperwork his attorney and friend, Brett Lincoln, had placed in front of him.

"Yes, it's what I *want* to do, but I'd be lying if I told you I didn't have doubts as to what's right for the company. Regardless, I've got to get out of here." Here, meaning Oklahoma. Unbeknownst to Dallas, Cash, Daisy or Georgina, Wyatt sat in Brett's high-rise Tulsa office, signing over the day-to-day running of the Buckhorn oil holdings to his more than capable second in command. Wyatt's degree was in geology, and he couldn't think of a more fitting way to get his head back in the proverbial game than to at least temporarily escape. Sooner the better.

He'd spend the next month or so tying up loose ends and then join forces with a major player in the oil exploration field in Ethiopia's Rift Valley basin. As part of their team, he'd break down geographical leads, checking everything from source rocks to possible hydrocarbon traps. The work would entail long, thankless hours in miserable conditions. Wyatt couldn't wait. The task could take years. As far as he was concerned, it could take forever.

Now, his only problem was telling his mother he wouldn't be home for Christmas.

"WE MEET AGAIN." WYATT didn't remember Natalie having such amazing curves in all the right places. But then, up until their epic kiss, he hadn't much thought of her at all. They had always been casual friends. Nothing more.

"What brings you to Weed Gulch Elementary on such a gorgeous Saturday morning?" she asked.

"Truth?" he asked with a contagious grin, setting a box loaded with donated goods on one of the tables designated for the day's rummage sale. "Mom's more than a little miffed with me, so I'm worming my way back into her good graces by doing her grunt work." In the week since meeting with Brett, he'd let his family in on his decision to leave. Not only were they all less than thrilled, his mother in particular was flipping out. Apparently, she had no desire for one of her *babies* to spend a few years in Ethiopia. Go figure.

Eyeing the still-full load in the back of his pickup, Natalie noted, "You must've been really bad to warrant hauling all of that. Doesn't she have employees for that sort of thing?"

"Sure, but at the moment, she thinks more of them than me."

"Ouch."

"Tell me about it. I even got wrangled into helping at the Halloween blowout she and Josie are having."

"Me, too," she said with a wince. "I'm already tired."

He laughed, surprised by how easy it was to shoot the breeze with his old friend.

"Well—" she aimed a thumb toward the kitchen "—I should probably let you unload. I've been assigned to brew coffee."

Hands in his pockets, he nodded. "Sounds good. Nice talking to you."

"Likewise," she said with a backward wave.

Fifteen minutes later, the time it took Wyatt to haul all his stuff to its assigned places, Natalie had returned, bearing a coffee urn so tall she could barely see around it.

"Let me give you a hand." Wyatt took it from her, carrying it to the area designated for a bake sale.

"Thanks." She trailed after him. "That thing turned out to be a lot heavier than it looked."

"What are you all raising money for?" he asked, for some unknown reason not wanting to say goodbye.

"Art and P.E. supplies. Our funding is perilously low. We barely have money for necessities like textbooks and paper, let alone the parts of school kids especially enjoy."

"Sounds like a great cause," he said. "Having always been a patron of the arts, I'll cut you a check."

She cocked her head, "Wyatt Buckhorn, last I remember of you in art class was when you and Owen glued everyone's colored pencils to their desks."

"That was my experimental art phase. It turned out bad. Now, I'm more into the classics."

Their shared laugh was nice. Comforting in an odd sort of way. Around Natalie, he'd always been able to be himself. With none of the usual guy/girl chemistry, there'd also never been drama. Granted, their kiss had hardly been tame, but it had been an isolated, one-time thing.

"Right," she teased. "Like the classic time you and Owen painted Claremore High's concrete zebra with purple and pink stripes?"

"Exactly. See?" he said with a playful nudge. "This generation could learn a lot from an artistic genius like me."

She rolled her eyes. "At the moment, they could learn more from your muscles. Want to help lug the cooler and milk?"

"If you'll admit what a great stunt that zebra bit was."

The grin she shot his way turned his insides to mush. Had she always been so pretty? "Since there aren't any impressionable young minds around, I'll admit our rival's zebra never looked better, but if you tell anyone I said that, I'll deny it."

"Whatever." He answered her grin with one of his own. "Show me what you want me to carry."

Following her into the school, Wyatt couldn't help but wonder if her backside had always been so juicy.

In the massive school kitchen, they filled a cooler with ice and kid-size cartons of milk. Wyatt carried it outside, Natalie beside him with napkins and a huge bowl of apples.

Midway down the school's front hall, Natalie tripped. As she went down, so did the apples, rolling in bursts of red, followed by an elegant snow of napkins.

"You okay?" Instantly by Natalie's side, Wyatt set down his load to help her.

"I think so," she managed through a messy sniffle. Crying? Over a few apples? "B-but I made a huge mess

and the PTA president is waiting for all of this and—
and—"

"Hey…" Cautious in his approach, he eased behind
her, awkwardly patting her back. "In case you missed
the memo, you shouldn't cry over spilled milk or
apples."

"I—I know," she said, laughing through more tears
while taking a tissue from her pocket to blow her nose.
"But lately, everything seems to be going wrong and
all I wanted to do this morning was sleep in, but I love
helping out with events like this, but I'm so tired and
emotional and all because I'm…" Rather than finishing her sentence, she waved her hands around as if announcing her next batch of tears.

"You're what?" he pressed, more than a little concerned by her uncharacteristic emotional meltdown.
"Sick? You don't have cancer, or anything, do you?"

"N-no." Her answer launched a fresh round of wails.
"I—I'm pregnant."

As if she'd delivered a physical blow, Wyatt recoiled.
"Pregnant?"

She nodded.

"Wow. Ah, I guess congratulations are in order."

"Thanks." Though she'd stopped crying, her voice
sounded defeated. "Could you please help me with this
mess? The apples are going to have to be rewashed."
On her knees, she gathered all of the nearby fruit and
napkins.

"Sure." Her condition had nothing to do with him,
so why were Wyatt's eyes now stinging? Things like
this—random reminders of his own shortcomings as
a man—were why he had to get out of Weed Gulch.
At times, it seemed as if the whole damned town was
turning up in this condition.

Just after Dallas's evil twins, Betsy and Bonnie, had been born and their mother, Bobbie Jo, had died, Wyatt suffered his own near death with a hellish bout of mumps. At the time, he'd been holed up in a dorm on an Alaskan North Slope drilling field, knowing there was no medical cure. So he'd stayed in his room, doing his damnedest not to infect others. Best he could figure, he'd caught it from a suspiciously snotty kid at Fairbanks International. A few months ago, during a routine physical, he'd mentioned the incident to Doc Haven, who in turn had worried aloud about the disease being a cause of male infertility. Always having assumed he'd one day have a big family, Wyatt opted to have his "equipment" tested.

Bad call.

Ever since, he'd felt like less a man.

The more babies his brothers and sister had, the more of an outsider he'd become. He'd tried to forget about the fact that he'd never have what they had. He'd tried to forget with willing women like Starla. It hadn't worked.

Now, with Natalie's *joyous* news, Wyatt's own inadequacies once again slapped him in the face.

"Think we got 'em all," he said once her load had been reassembled. "But how about you find a nice place to sit down, and I'll get this stuff outside."

"I appreciate the offer, but I'm good. My ego's more bruised than my body. Sorry about flipping out on you like that."

"No problem," he said on the return trip to the kitchen. "We all have our moments."

Standing alongside her at one of the kitchen's commercial sinks, Wyatt couldn't stop his mind from racing. He should be home, studying geographical charts. Instead, he wanted to know if that UPS dude Natalie had been dating was her baby's father. If so, why wasn't he here with her today? Where had he been at the christening? Had she mentioned they'd had a fight? Most of all, Wyatt wondered why he cared.

He'd known Natalie forever, yet it was funny how when it came right down to it, they hardly knew each other at all. Not the way it mattered. "You and your baby's father tying the knot?"

"Nope." She quickened her pace, in the process dropping the fruit she'd been trying to wash.

"But you two have been together for a long time. What's the problem?"

Upon placing the last apple in the bowl, she turned off the water. "Short story, Craig had no interest in becoming a father."

"What the hell?" What was wrong with that guy? Here, Wyatt would've given anything to have his own son or daughter, yet the loser Natalie had hooked up with was running away?

How is that any different from what you're doing?

The thought stung. But Wyatt knew damn well his reason for leaving was far from cowardly. He wasn't so much shirking responsibility as chasing self-preservation.

The faint grin tugging the corners of her pretty lips contained the sadness of an abandoned basket of kittens. "Yeah, *what the hell* pretty much sums it up. Craig initially tried the whole commitment thing, but in the end said he wasn't ready to be a father and that was that."

"For what it's worth," Wyatt said, "I'm sorry."

She shrugged. "Thanks, but I'll be fine."

"I get that, but you shouldn't have to just be fine.

You should be over-the-moon happy." Wyatt couldn't imagine the joy he'd feel were he in this Craig character's position. His heart would feel so full it'd hurt. Thing is, he'd never get the chance.

"Really," Natalie said, "I've got this whole single-mom thing figured out. Sort of," she tagged on with a sad little laugh.

"Aw, you're going to make a great mother." Wyatt abandoned the napkins he'd been straightening to give her a hug. In his arms, she felt small and fragile. The man in him wanted nothing more than to protect her and make everything okay. She smelled of sweet apples and barely there floral perfume. She reminded him of the kind of take-home-to-mom girl he'd always planned to marry—at least until fate had thrown him a screw-you curveball. Now, no kids. No marriage. No life he'd always imagined.

"LADIES…" WYATT TIPPED his cowboy hat.

"Hey." Was it wrong that a simple grin from the man had Natalie ready to swoon? The Buckhorn Halloween extravaganza was in full swing, and the chilly night air came as a welcome reprieve to the stuffy, kid-loaded barn.

"You're just in time," Josie said to Wyatt. "If we're going to keep to Georgina's schedule, we need to hitch the horses to the wagon ASAP."

"Yes, ma'am." He gave his sister-in-law a salute, but Natalie received a wink. Oh, she knew full well he was just playing around, but the gesture returned her fertile imagination to that epic kiss, compounded by his small kindnesses at the school rummage sale. For all the years they'd been acquaintances, she was only just now seeing what an asset he'd be as a true friend.

While Wyatt set about readying their ride, Josie returned to the party, leaving Natalie on her own with the man. And his dizzingly well-fitting jeans. Even in the dark, his size was impressive. Tall and broad in all the right places. Their kiss had also educated her on the full extent of his strong muscles.

Mouth dry, she looked away, disappointed in herself by the realization she'd been staring.

"It's okay," he said, leading a large draft. "You'd be a fool not to look."

"Excuse me?"

"You know you like what you see." After another wink, he smacked his butt.

"You're nuts." Natalie tried playing it cool, but instead, burst out laughing. "And annoyingly handsome."

"Thanks." He cinched the horse's lead. "I was just thinking the same about you. Only with more feminine adjectives."

Their banter was all in good fun, but as Wyatt returned to his task and Natalie busied herself helping two dozen children and a few parents onto the wagon, she couldn't help but reflect on how differently her life might have been if Craig hadn't turned out to be such a flake. But then it wasn't all Craig's fault she'd ended up pregnant.

The few times he had forgotten a condom, she could've stopped their lovemaking. But honestly, she'd secretly hoped to become pregnant. She'd foolheartedly believed a baby would magically drive Craig to the altar. Oh—it'd driven him all right, straight to the nearest highway out of the state.

With the wagon jolting to a start, surrounded by sweet-smelling hay and singing children, stars twinkling above, Natalie choked back a sudden yearning.

For all of her brave talk to Josie about how she'd be fine raising her baby on her own, she didn't want to.

In the dark shadows she drank in Wyatt's strong profile, imagining him with her in a more simple time. In Oklahoma a hundred years earlier. Wyatt was a man's man. She could all too easily see him leading a cattle drive down the Chisholm Trail. He might handle the oil side of the family business now, but in high school, he and Dallas had often been hired by her father to help with their cattle. As a little kid, Wyatt's favorite game at recess had been wagon train.

Too bad her imagination was the only place any of them were perfect. For all of Wyatt's physical attributes, when it came to how he treated women, Wyatt was no different than Craig. Oh sure, he might be far more smooth, but his basic noncommitment routine was much the same. Maybe worse—at least Craig had told Natalie to her face he was done. Wyatt's kissing stunt had forced Starla to do the work.

The only reason Wyatt treated Natalie with respectful kid gloves was the knowledge that they would never be more than friends, never mind the glimpse of chemistry they'd shared.

"Miss Natalie," seven-year-old Bonnie Buckhorn said, "I thought you were s'posed to tell us a ghost story?"

"Yeah." Bonnie's twin, Betsy, climbed onto Natalie's lap. "And if you don't tell the story, then when Uncle Cash jumps out in his costume, trying to scare us, then nobody's gonna be scared."

"Hush," Natalie halfheartedly scolded. "That's supposed to be a surprise for your friends."

Betsy folded her chubby arms. "Then Daddy

shouldn't've been talking so loud with Grandma, because I know all about it."

Laughing, Natalie gave the pint-size know-it-all a squeeze. Was it wrong to pray her child wasn't quite as precocious?

By the time the story had ended and all of the kids save for Betsy were sufficiently spooked, Wyatt pulled the wagon alongside the old stone mill where a bonfire crackled. Dancing flames only added to the already ghoulish scene. Gnarled oak limbs cast monster shadows held at bay with plenty of marshmallows, chocolate and laughter.

Natalie had just assembled a giant s'more when a couple of Bonnie's masked friends ran into her during a ghost-hunter chase. They apologized, but only after having caused Natalie to fall.

"Lord, woman…" Wyatt sprung from the crowd gathered around the fire to help her to her feet. From there, with surprising tenderness, he brushed gravel from her palms. His warmth came as a shock, causing her breath to hitch. Awareness of his size, his strength, the decadence of melted chocolate on his breath, melded into a confused knot in her chest. Was she coming down with something? "There you go," he said. "All better. Damned kids. Should've watched where they were going. But you need to be careful. This is starting to be a habit."

"Th-thanks." He released her hands, but not her gaze. Which, if only for a few seconds, was too intense.

He looked away before asking, "Is the rest of you all right? You know, like the baby?"

Natalie nodded. "I think so."

"Good." Hands in his pockets, he looked to the sky, then the wagon. "Well, I should check on the horses."

Just like that, Wyatt was gone.

Natalie should've been fine with his leaving, but oddly enough, she felt lonely.

"WHAT WAS THAT ABOUT?" Dallas asked.

"What do you mean?" Wyatt checked the horse's harnesses.

"That thing with Nat. You're not thinking of starting something with her, are you? In case you forgot, you're breaking your mother's heart in just under a month."

Wyatt shot his brother a dirty look. "For the record, your daughter's hellion friends knocked Nat down. I was doing a good deed. As for Mom, with as many rug rats as you've got running around the ranch, she'll never notice I'm gone."

"Trust me, she'll notice. She already asked if she should hire a bodyguard for you in case your trip gets dicey. Don't know why you can't just stick around here and pop out some grandkids for her like the rest of us. Would that be so hard?" Stroking one of the horse's cheeks, no doubt when he thought Wyatt wasn't looking, Dallas rechecked the harnesses. Classic Dallas. Always in his business. Never trusting Wyatt to competently handle a job. Ignoring the fact that since Wyatt had taken over the oil side of the ranch, they'd made money hand over fist. Ever since his big brother had the twins, he'd seemed to equate success with the number of kids a guy had. Considering his own shortcomings in that field, Wyatt figured he'd had just about all of his brother's wisdom he could handle.

Wyatt said, "How about I take the truck back to my place and you handle the wagon?"

"Won't work," Dallas said. "We need you here to—"

"How about making it work." Beyond angry, Wyatt

strode to the vehicle. Nine times out of ten, Dallas left the keys in the ignition.

This time was no exception.

Wyatt started the engine, hit the lights then bucked it into gear, in the process damn near hitting Natalie.

"Where are you going?" she called over the ancient V-8.

"Home. Had enough family togetherness to last the next year."

"Me, too," she said, fumbling with her fingers at her waist. Had it always been huge? How could he not have noticed? "Would you mind taking me to my car?"

For a split second, Wyatt thought about turning her down, but then his mind flashed on just how pleasant his past couple meetings with her had been. Natalie was the anti-Dallas.

Meeting his brother's glare, Wyatt said to Natalie, "Hop in. Let's go lookin' for trouble."

Chapter Three

"What was that about?" Natalie asked once they were well away from the bonfire's glow.

"You really don't wanna know."

"Wouldn't have asked if I didn't." She rolled down her window. Sweet wood smoke laced the air rushing across her flushed cheeks and chest. "Your mom, bless her heart, just pressed my hot button nine ways to Sunday. Way I see it, I'll tell you my frustrations, then you can vent yours."

"Deal. Do you like shooting?"

Forehead furrowed, she angled on the seat to face him. "Haven't done it since I was a kid, but it was fun then."

"Oh," he said with a sharp laugh, "you're gonna love this."

Twenty minutes driving across dark prairie landed them alongside an old wood outbuilding and trash pile from the land's previous owners. One of the latest parcels added to the vast Buckhorn spread, the old Spring place wasn't fancy, but according to Josie, Dallas had gone after it with a vengeance.

"Come on," Wyatt said, taking a 30-30 rifle from

the back window. "And grab the shells from the glove box."

Moonlight shimmered off a pond. From some-where—Natalie hoped far away—coyotes yipped. After handing Wyatt the ammo, she hugged herself to ward off a chill.

"Cold?" he asked, boots crunching on hard-packed dirt.

"A little."

He removed his ranch coat, settling it about her shoulders. It was still warm and smelled of him—a de-licious blend of leather and soap and citrus that quick-ened her pulse.

"Thanks."

He cast her a faint, unreadable smile before fishing rusty cans from a burn barrel. After lining ten along the crooked posts of a barbwire fence, he took the rifle from under his arm and the shells from his back pocket and loaded the gun.

Handing it to her, he said, "Ladies first."

"I appreciate the sentiment," she said, "but it's been a while. As a refresher course, I'll watch you a few times."

Shrugging, he said, "Suit yourself. I've got to work some of this frustration out before I say something to Dallas I'm gonna regret." Aiming at the farthest can, he fired, blowing it to smithereens. "Damn! Now that's what I'm talking about."

Natalie laughed above her still-ringing ears. "Hand me that gun, cowboy. Training camp's over. I want a turn."

He loaded it before handing it to her. "You sure you know what you're doing?"

"No, but how hard can it be?" She prepared to fire, but he stopped her.

"A pose like that is going to give you one helluva bruise. Try this…" Behind her, he drew back the butt of the rifle, landing it square against her shoulder. His proximity set off explosions that had nothing to do with gun powder. The tall, lean length of him radiated heat to her shoulders and back and butt, igniting a tingling swirl in her belly. What was wrong with her? She'd never been attracted to Wyatt. He was the kind of guy she knew she could count on if she had a flat tire. He wasn't the kind of guy a single, pregnant woman turned to for a rebound fling. He was renowned for breaking hearts—never saving them. "Feel better?"

With his warm breath in her ear, she most certainly did not feel better. What she truly felt was a yearning hunger for another kiss. Ludicrous, but undeniable. Forcing a breath, she nodded.

"Good. Line the can in your sight, then *pow.* Blow all your frustrations away." He'd whispered that one little word, causing more damage to her resolve to resist his charm than she'd ever do to the can.

"This one's for you, Georgina."

"Sounds intriguing," he teased.

She pulled the trigger, and found that the noise and thrill were just the ticket to clearing the angst buildup.

An hour later, having finished off the box of shells, Natalie sat alongside Wyatt in the old truck, warming her hands in front of blowing heater vents. "Thanks for this. It turned out to be exactly what I needed."

"Happy to oblige."

After a few moments' comfortable silence, co-cooned in the truck's dark cab, Natalie said, "I haven't yet found the nerve to tell my folks about my pregnancy. Their world's pretty black and white, and having an unwed daughter with a baby on the way wouldn't even begin to compute."

"Sorry. When it comes to family disapproval, mine wrote the book."

"Oh, please." Twisting on the seat for a better view of his handsome profile, she asked, "What have you ever done that the mighty Buckhorns disapproved of?"

"Like your folks," he said, narrowly avoiding a fallen tree, "they would prefer I be married. Oh—and they can't stand my house."

"Really? Town gossip says it's pretty amazing."

"I like to think so." His smile warmed her far more efficiently that the heater.

"And lately, they're mighty pissed about me leaving."

"Hmm…Josie told me about your great Ethiopian adventure. Sounds like a once-in-a-lifetime chance. Something to be done before you finally do settle down with a wife and those requisite 2.5 kids."

Natalie had expected Wyatt to appreciate her support. Instead, his expression hardened.

She asked, "Did I somehow offend you?"

He shook his head and gripped the wheel tighter.

"Then why the one-eighty in your mood?"

After a glance out his window at the inky nothing beyond the glass, he exhaled. "What the hell? I've needed to get this off my chest for a while now, and I like you, Natalie. Always have. Most girls fell for my Buckhorn hype, but not you. You always treated me like a regular Joe."

Stomach sour, Natalie wasn't sure she wanted to hear whatever Wyatt had to say.

"I appreciate that. Outside of family, and a few close

friends, there aren't a lot of people I can trust to keep my private issues private. Know what I mean?"

She nodded. "I feel that way about Josie. As happy as I was to see her marry Dallas, part of me mourned to have lost her. Sure, we'll always be close, but not the way we were before she began bursting with family."

Wincing, he said, "There's that word again. The bane of my existence."

"Family?" Wrinkling her nose, she said, "I would think however your relatives are, they're still your blood and you love them."

"Love has nothing to do with it. Their expectations for me to be just like them is what brings me down—especially since no matter how much they bitch and nag about me marrying and having kids, their hopes will never come to pass."

"Why? You're young. How can you arbitrarily decide you never want to be more than a bachelor?"

"Easy." Thumping the heel of his hand against the wheel, he added, "Especially since it wasn't even my decision. I'll never have a son or daughter."

"What do you mean?"

"To spell it out, I'm sterile."

Heart aching for him, eyes stinging with tears she struggled to hold in, she asked, "H-how do you know?"

"Nasty case of mumps. Doc Haven tested me. That's why I'm so desperate to get out of Weed Gulch. No one knows, and the last thing I want to do is tell them. I don't want their pity or well-meaning lectures on the wonders of adoption. I need to be left alone, you know? Just come to grips with this in my own way."

Hand on his forearm, she asked, "How long have you known?"

"A few months, and damned if the more kids my

brothers and sister pop out, the more disconnected I feel. I will forever be the lone man out and it—"

When his voice cracked, Natalie scooted across the seat to put her arms around him.

He stopped the truck, killing the engine.

Though Wyatt never shed a tear, Natalie could only imagine how much his diagnosis had hurt. For a guy like him, his macho manliness no doubt meant the world. To never be able to have his own namesake must be crushing.

"I'm so sorry," she said, holding him for all she was worth. "Ironic how your family wants nothing more than for you to produce a child, and mine is going to be peeved for that very fact."

"Which is why I need to get the hell out of Dodge. For the most part, family is great, but this is one time when I just want to escape."

Not sure what the politically correct thing to say was at a time like this, Natalie said the first thing that popped into her mind. "I don't blame you. The Buckhorns are a pretty intense bunch. I can just imagine Georgina catching wind of this. Demanding you have every test in the book done, ignoring the fact that you're a big boy and no doubt already double- and triple-checked this for yourself."

"True."

She gave him another hug. "You go off on this adventure of yours, and once you get back, maybe you'll feel better about your lot, maybe you won't, but at least you'll be out there, living life to its fullest."

Easing back, he said, "You're amazing. How is it I never dated you?"

"Simple," she teased, "I'm too smart to ever fall victim to your charm."

ONE WEEK LATER, FIVE rows from Weed Gulch Elementary's stage, Wyatt sat crammed between his sister-in-law Wren and his nephew Kolt. Wren's nearly three-year-old daughter, Robin, sat on her lap, smelling like she might be having an issue with whatever she'd eaten for dinner. Trapped in a room bursting with families, Wyatt had never been more keenly aware of his own deficiency.

The one person who'd made him feel better about himself and his decision to leave town was Natalie.

Daisy's dark-haired eleven-year-old son, Kolt, wrinkled his nose. "Aunt Wren, Robin *really* stinks."

Just then Natalie stepped out from behind the blue velvet stage curtains. Natalie was the night's MC. She looked good in a rusty-orange sweater over brown pants. He liked her hair, too. Loose and wavy. Pretty— like her smile.

Cash's wife, Wren, laughed. "I know, hon. I told your uncle to not feed her bean soup, but he didn't listen. She's almost totally potty trained, but not good enough for that much fiber."

"Shhh." Weary of baby talk, eagerly awaiting whatever Natalie was about to say, Wyatt crossed his arms and prayed for the family portion of the night to end.

"What a wonderful turnout!" Natalie said with a bright smile. Had she always looked so good? "On behalf of our students and staff, thank you for taking time to attend our fall concert. The kids have worked hard, and can't wait to show off their skills."

Once the program started, Wyatt had to admit all of the songs and hand motions were cute, but instead of focusing on his nieces' talent, he felt trapped under his own dark cloud. How different would the night be were he watching his own children perform?

The show droned on for two hours, during which every baby and toddler present screamed in turns. By the time the twins took their last bows, Wyatt was more than ready to bolt. But no. First, he had to have cake and punch in the deafening cafeteria. Why, why hadn't he driven himself?

"Not that you probably deserve it," teased a warm, familiar voice from beside him, "but come on. You look like a man in dire need of silence." Natalie led Wyatt by his arm out of the chaos and into the bliss of her deserted office. She gestured for him to take a seat on the sofa. She parked behind her desk.

Hands to his throbbing forehead, Wyatt asked, "How do you stand being around here all day, every day?"

"It's usually not this crazy. When school's in session, rules and procedures keep the noise to a minimum."

"Still…" He managed a grimace. "I'm starting to loathe kids. Which in my case is a good thing, right?"

"Oh, stop." Tidying a pile of papers, she added, "The night hasn't been that bad. And anyway, it's over now." Natalie looked awfully grown-up seated behind her big desk. How many crying kiddos had been in here for her to soothe?

He sat a little straighter.

She reached for an apple-shaped candy dish mounded with Hershey's Kisses. "Want one?"

Shaking his head, he said, "I'm maxed out on sugar."

Apparently she wasn't, as she proceeded to unwrap three of the treats before popping them in her mouth. Her expression was one of pure pleasure. Damned if she didn't look in the throes of an orgasm. The notion produced pressure beneath his fly, along with the asinine urge to lick a speck of chocolate from the corner of her lips.

Wyatt cleared his throat. "I, ah, wasn't going to come tonight."

"Why?" Was she aware that when she leaned forward, resting her elbows on her desk, her shadowy cleavage popped into view? "This was a big deal for the twins. I know they wanted their favorite uncle here."

Wyatt snorted. "Cash is everyone's favorite."

"Don't sell yourself short. The girls talk about you all the time. Bonnie refers to you as her favorite oil king."

"Nice," he said with a chuckle. After taking one of her candies, he added, "My Ethiopian residence card came today."

"Are you excited?"

"Yes and no. As much as I'll be relieved to get out of here, it's strange to think the next time I see Esther, she'll be walking."

"How does that make you feel? Any regrets?"

He took more candy. Had Natalie always smelled so good? Like a mix of flowers and chocolate and the faintest hint of a just-sharpened pencil?

"Wyatt?" she asked, waving her hand in front of his face. "Earth to Wyatt."

"Huh?"

"I asked if any part of you regrets leaving."

Funny, but at the moment, the one thing Wyatt knew he'd miss about Weed Gulch was Natalie. His whole life she'd been right under his nose. How could he have not taken the time to know her before now? "Other than hot and cold running water, electricity and reliable meals, I think I'm good."

She laughed, which made him smile, too.

Which was nice. If only for a little while.

"Is Wyatt here?" On Saturday morning, Natalie had found a travel book on Ethiopia at a yard sale. Hoping she'd run into Wyatt at Georgina's latest gathering on Sunday afternoon, she'd brought it along.

"No," his mother said, "he hasn't even left the county lines, but for all the time he spends with me, he might as well already be gone." Georgina, dressed in a Victorian period costume complete with a huge feathered hat, daintily sipped her chamomile tea. While all of the ladies present looked to be enjoying high tea, Cash and Dallas had holed up in the movie room. The mere thought of manly Wyatt eating *petit fours* and discussing the perfect Thanksgiving side dishes brought on a smile. "He said he had business in Tulsa, but I was up all night and this morning with indigestion and never saw him leave."

"Hmm…" Natalie hid behind her orange spice.

Truth was, she hardly knew him well enough on a personal level to be disappointed by not seeing him today, so why did she now feel pouty? She'd been looking forward to giving him her gift. She'd never met anyone brave enough to just pack up and run away. Sure, lots of people talked about it, but Wyatt had the balls to actually do it. She admired him for that. And as anxious as she was about tackling the frontier of single-motherhood, she planned on adopting Wyatt's fearless attitude when it came to raising her child.

"I'm tired of talking about my horrible son," Georgina said above a classical crescendo, "let's talk about you. I'm concerned. I spoke with your mom the other day at gardening club and she said she's afraid you're hiding something from her."

Natalie lightly shook her head. "Mrs. Buckhorn, I don't mean to be rude, but my personal, private business aside, you just called your son horrible for following his heart. I don't mean any disrespect, but as the one woman in his life he loves above all others, shouldn't you support his decision?"

"It's not that simple." Georgina set her cup and saucer on the table. "We need Wyatt here. His leaving is selfish. *I* need him here."

"For what? From what he's told me, he's set up your oil holdings to practically run themselves."

The older woman sighed. "Your frown tells me you don't understand. My kind of clarity on these matters only comes with age."

To be polite Natalie nodded, while inside, she vowed to never be so far removed from her son or daughter to stop communicating with them not just on the daily superficial matters, but on issues that truly matter.

Fed up with small talk and hearing advice on everything from getting Craig back to shedding those few extra pounds she seemed to have put on, Natalie didn't bother consulting Josie before sneaking out the back door.

Cold November rain hitting her cheeks came as a welcome relief. As did the sweet smell of a wood fire. The house had been stifling. Too much perfume fighting for attention.

Once in her car, for the longest time Natalie rested her forehead against the wheel. What was wrong with the people of this town that they all felt not only obliged to share their opinions on the most personal aspects of her life, but downright entitled?

Wyatt was right to leave. If she hadn't gone and done a stupid thing like believing Craig loved her, she might still be in a position to do some running herself. As it was, she couldn't afford to abandon her job or support system—no matter how annoying they all might be.

Backing out of her parking space, Natalie had just decided to make an emergency ice-cream run when it occurred to her that maybe an even better way to spend her afternoon would be by talking out her frustrations about Georgina with the only other person who seemed equally annoyed by her pushy manner—Wyatt.

Before chickening out, instead of aiming her car for the main road, she steered down the blacktop lane leading to his home. In all the years she'd known the Buckhorns, she'd never seen Wyatt's house. Come to think of it, not that many folks around town had.

Cash and Wren lived in a clean-lined home not half a mile from Georgina. Josie and Dallas lived with the Buckhorn matriarch in the main house, and Daisy and Luke resided in Luke's cabin until renovations were finished on the historic wreck they were lovingly restoring. Wyatt, however, resided in the woods. Reportedly a good ten miles from the rest of the clan. Rumor had him living in everything from a tin shed to a mobile home to a playboy-style mansion.

Three miles into her trek, rain drummed her car roof. Poor visibility had her slowing to a ridiculous pace. Mile after mile, the blacktop road snaked through dense forest. Just when Natalie was convinced she must have driven all the way to Kansas, there it was. Wyatt's house. Only town gossip hadn't done it justice.

Like the oil rigs he spent most of his time working, the structure was steel, clinging to a wooded hillside.

At first glance, a haphazard series of staggered boxes. Upon closer inspection, the hard metal bones had been covered in glass skin that even on such a dreary day, reflected forest and sky. The place was spellbinding. All the more so when through one of the center panels she spied Wyatt lounging on a couch, watching TV.

Parking alongside his black truck with its Buckhorn Ranch insignia on the doors, she left her purse in the car, struggling instead with an umbrella and his book.

At the end of a gray flagstone walk, she faced an imposing, cranberry-red door. Dripping, trying to keep her umbrella from flying away in the wind, she was on the verge of bailing on her impromptu mission, when the door opened and there stood Wyatt. Bare-chested, wearing faded jeans and nothing else.

"Thought I heard a car. What're you doing here?"

"Nice to see you, too." Leaving her umbrella, she brushed past him.

"Sorry. I didn't mean that to come out the way it sounded. Guess I'm surprised to see you. Thought you'd be holed up with my family all day."

"I was—for most of it, anyway. Then your mother ticked me off, and I just wanted out."

"What'd she do now?"

"I'll tell you just as soon as you show me where the nearest bathroom is," she said, her teeth chattering.

He pointed down a shadowy hall. "First door on your left."

Natalie finished with the necessities that her pregnancy had created and took one look in the mirror and cringed. The humidity had transformed her formerly straightened long hair into a frizz ball. Her mascara ran, and her complexion sported a vampire pall. If she'd brought in her purse, she'd have at least had a ponytail holder to tame her hair. As it was, she settled for using tissue to fix her face.

"Took you long enough." Wyatt hadn't left the entry hall.

"Are you the bathroom police?"

His white-toothed grin stole her breath. "I've seen feral cats look better than you."

"If I had the energy, I'd beat you to a pulp."

"Yeah, right." He helped her remove her coat. "You tried once in fourth grade and failed miserably."

"Only because Dallas came to your rescue."

"That could be debated." He tossed her coat onto an antique sideboard. The eclectic mix of furniture was genius. Had he done it himself or had help?

"Come on." Taking her by her arm, he said, "Let's get you warmed up." He led her down a short flight of stairs to a room so awe-inspiring she literally couldn't think of a single intelligent thing to say. Three walls were composed of floor-to-ceiling glass. Centered on the furthest wall was a river-stone fireplace, glowing with warmth. A mammoth plasma-screen TV hung above the mantel and a custom U-shaped sectional occupied the center of the cathedral-ceilinged space. A sumptuous white area rug covered maple floors. The overall effect was as if they were floating through the forest on a magic carpet.

"I shouldn't be here." Natalie nodded to her still damp clothes and specks of mud on her shoes. "I'll muss something."

Kneeling alongside her, he removed one of her black heels, then the other. His knuckles grazed her ankles, shocking her with the unexpected intimacy of his touch. "Next excuse?"

"Th-thanks." Her teeth still occasionally chattered,

but she suspected now more because of her erratic pulse than cold. His actions had been kind. Something Josie might've done—only with plenty of teasing and a goofy smile.

"No problem." Taking the TV remote from the sofa, he muted a football game. "Coffee? Have a seat and I'll put on a fresh pot."

"Thanks, but—" she pointed to the bump beneath her billowy blue blouse "—no caffeine for me."

"Right. I forgot." Hands in his pockets, he looked to the floor, then met her gaze. "Ironic, isn't it?"

"What?"

"You being pregnant. All the fertility around here is what's driving me to leave. A wise man wouldn't have let you in this house."

"What's that make you?" She couldn't resist zinging back.

"Ouch." His smile blocked all rational thought. "Guess that makes me not-so-wise, but seriously, it's nice to see you."

"Likewise." They shared an awkward moment of silence, gazes meeting, then breaking, only to meet up again. Unable to cope with her awareness of his size, and how easy it was to recall every detail of their kiss, she struggled to remember her reason for being at his home. "I, um, brought you a book, but left it in the bathroom." Hitching her thumb that way, she said, "I'll go get it."

"Let me," he said, already halfway there. "You have a seat."

She did, but mostly because of her rubbery knees than because he'd asked.

"This is great," he called from the hall. Entering the living room, he flipped through the glossy pages.

"I ordered one online, but it hasn't come. Where'd you find it?"

"Yard sale. It was only a quarter, but I thought you might enjoy thumbing through."

"I will. Thanks. Ethiopia doesn't get a lot of coverage on travel sites."

"Are you afraid of violence?"

"I'd be lying if I said I wasn't. I'll be working with a major oil player, though, so there will be security." He sat on the opposite end of the sofa to her, still leafing through his gift. "The poverty aspect is tough, too. It bothers me that we'll have the latest in gadgetry and freeze-dried gourmet when the locals are barely scraping by. But then on the flip side, our base camp is set up at a safari resort. Up until researching this trip, I never would've thought anyone went to Ethiopia on vacation. Turns out it's a beautiful country."

"Hmm…" Reflective, with her hand over her tummy, Natalie said, "All in all, it still sounds like a wonderful adventure, which is why I'm so miffed with your mom. She called you horrible and selfish for leaving."

His only reaction was to shrug. "She's told me her opinion to my face. At first, it stung. Now, I'm over it."

"Still… Have you considered letting her in on your reasons for leaving?"

"Next topic." He added a couple logs to the fire. "In general, how was the party?"

"The usual. Over-the-top food, decorations and conversation. When I left, Daisy was counting how many times she'd seen contractor 'cracks' at her new house. They had to tear down the new north wing and start over."

He winced. "Makes me doubly glad I missed it."

"If you don't mind my asking," she said, "why didn't you at least want to spend time with your brothers?"

Stretching out his legs and crossing them at the ankles, he took his sweet time to answer. "Suffice to say it's complicated."

"I do have my master's in counseling."

He snorted. "That your not-so-subtle way of comparing my brainpower to that of a third grader?"

"Wyatt, I'm serious." Though the rain outside fell harder, his complexion appeared red and overheated. "I get that your issues must be like a slow death inside, but you can't run forever—well, you could, but you'd miss out on a lot."

"Master's or not," he said, "feel free to drop it. You're making me wish I'd never told you."

"Sorry."

"Are you?" he snapped. "You sit there judging me when you already have the one gift I never will. Think about it."

Throat tight, Natalie sighed. She slipped on her shoes and coat and made it all the way to the door without him saying a word.

She'd just stepped back out in the rain when Wyatt called, "Hey, Nat?"

"Yes?" Was it wrong for her to hope he'd repair the gaping hole now between them?

"Thanks again for the book, but it's probably best you don't come around anymore."

Chapter Four

"Look how big you're getting."

Thanksgiving morning, Wyatt glanced over his shoulder as he crouched in front of his mother's fireplace. Josie patted Natalie's growing baby bump and for whatever reason, the sight irked the hell out of him. She hadn't been that pregnant last time he'd seen her, had she?

"I know." Natalie raised her shirt to show off elastic-banded black slacks. "I had to go up a size in maternity pants. Suffice to say, my secret is completely out."

"You look adorable," Josie gushed. "Almost makes me want to have another baby."

Laughing, Natalie said, "You might want to consult Dallas about that."

As if he weren't even in the room, the two women chatted right past him. Just as well, Wyatt figured while he lit kindling in the hearth. His latest conversation with Natalie still stung. *Issues?* What the hell did she know about what he was going through? If she'd tried for years to have a baby, but kept miscarrying, would she find it enjoyable to hang with the most fertile family in Oklahoma?

Just as soon as his Thanksgiving duties were over,

he was heading to Tulsa. The Mayo Hotel had a rooftop bar. He'd get a room, a few drinks, meet a hot woman looking for a good time. With luck, they'd share fun and breakfast. Time to act like the eligible bachelor he was.

At dinner, his seven-year-old niece Bonnie turned to him and said, "Uncle Wyatt?"

"Yes, ma'am?" He helped himself to seconds of green bean casserole.

"Could you please cut my meat?" She held up a thick slice of turkey and waved it.

"Just eat it like that."

"I can't." She dredged her free fingers through gravy, then licked them like lollipops. "It's bad manners."

"And what you're doing isn't?" he asked.

Betsy, her twin, who sat on his other side, said, "She likes eating her gravy like that. Me, too."

"You guys are gross." Kolt sat across from them, looking ready to barf.

"Girls," Dallas warned, "remember what we talked about? Today is the perfect time for you to practice being respectful young ladies."

"Daddy," Betsy said, coating her stubby digits with more gravy, "me and Bonnie decided we just wanna be like regular us."

Josie passed the damp washcloth she'd used on two-year-old Mabel down the table to Wyatt. "Would you mind cleaning the twins? I'd hate for them to get gravy on their dresses."

"But I like it," Bonnie said. "And I'm big. I can wash my own hands."

"Be my guest." Wyatt handed the kid the cloth.

Dallas cast his younger brother a put-out glare

before pushing back his chair, snatching the cloth and wiping down the girls himself. "There. Now, eat with your fork, spoon and knife or you'll sit in the kitchen."

"You're mean," Bonnie said.

To Wyatt's way of thinking, the day being a holiday and all, Dallas was taking the whole table-manners thing too seriously. There had been a time when the twins would have been *painting* the walls with gravy, so their current behavior was already a vast improvement.

A glance to the far end of the table had Wyatt locking gazes with Natalie. She smiled, but it didn't reach her eyes. What was she thinking? Did she, too, want to add her two cents to the gravy debate or was her mind wandering to weightier matters? Maybe she wished she were seated alongside her baby's father, rather than being sandwiched between Josie and Daisy?

She'd been quick to fault him for his demons, but how much time did she spend worrying about her own?

"WHEW." JOSIE DROPPED TO the sofa. Daisy and Wren joined her. "That was tougher than I'd planned."

Natalie had gone along with them to put their menageries to bed. The twins and Kolt had been allowed to stay up late to watch a movie.

Daisy asked the men, "Have you all done anything productive today?"

"We cleaned up after dinner." Luke stretched and yawned. "Plus, I took Kolt and the baby to see my folks."

"I told you I would've gone." Daisy rounded the room picking up baby bibs and toys and blankets.

"And I told you," Luke said, "there was no use in

getting you riled up when you were having a nice day with your family."

"Is your mother ever going to forgive me?" Daisy dabbed a tissue at the corners of her eyes.

Luke went to her, circling her with his strong arms. "Last I recall, you married me and not my mom."

"Thank God," she said into his chest.

Struggling past a pang of jealousy for the deep connection Daisy and Luke shared, Natalie felt for Daisy. Yes, Daisy had done a terrible thing in keeping Kolt from his father for the first ten years of his life, but she'd had good reason. Luke had long since forgiven her. Why couldn't his mom?

When Natalie became a mother, she'd already picked up tips on what kind of parent she didn't want to be, but what would she stand for? She had no clue how to handle day-to-day feeding and diapering logistics, let alone the kinds of problems looming ahead of her when her baby started talking and walking and going to school. How much easier would her pregnancy be knowing her parents stood firmly in her corner?

"I've got a great idea." Josie's smile was supersized and suspicious. "How about we lighten the mood with a game? Trivial Pursuit? Pictionary? Charades?"

All present save for Dallas moaned.

"Count me out," Wyatt said.

"I should check the horses." Cash was already on his feet.

"If we play charades, I'm in," Daisy said, "but only if I'm paired with you, Josie. Dallas and Luke cheat."

Dallas waved off his sister's concern. "You're the cheater. Come on, Luke, let's show your wife how it's done."

"Yay!" Josie clapped. "I'll be right back with scratch paper, a basket and a couple of pens."

"Wanna be on my team?" Wren asked Cash. In her third year of residency, to save precious time and effort, she'd cut her long dark hair into an adorable pixie style. Judging by the heated looks and stolen kisses her husband had given her all day, he approved.

"Guess that leaves us." Wyatt crammed alongside Natalie on the love seat. Every brush of their forearms or thighs flip-flopped her stomach. Had to be hormones causing such havoc, because it certainly wasn't common sense. Not only was Wyatt soon to embark on a seriously long trek, even if he weren't, he would never be the right sort of guy for her and her baby. If Natalie ever dated again—which was a very big *if*— she'd look for the most committed man around. The kind of salt-of-the-earth guy who was so emotionally invested in living the rest of his life with her and her baby that he'd never even consider time spent without them.

"Nat, pick," Josie prodded, waving the basket with the movies they had to act out in front of her. They were playing by Buckhorn house rules, which meant the team who first guesses the film title they were acting out won the point.

"Sorry," Natalie said with a shake of her foggy head. She removed a folded card and by necessity, leaned closer to Wyatt to let him see *Raging Bull*.

"Here's how I think we should do this," he whispered in her ear. His breath was moist and hot and flavored with the sweet hint of pumpkin pie. Forearms covered in goose bumps, Natalie forced herself to focus. "I'm going to play a bull, charging at you. But

I'll be angry. You act scared, like you're trying to get out of the way. Make sense?"

"Uh-huh." How was it possible for a man to smell so good? Especially one she no longer even especially liked!

He stood first, offering her his hand to help her to her feet. As was starting to be the norm, electricity sizzled between them. A bad thing, considering their current level of tension. She hadn't intended to drill him that afternoon at his house, but she stood by what she said. Maybe not in the near future, but one day, she believed Wyatt would regret his life spent running. A little adventure was fine, but a steady diet of chocolate eventually led to indigestion.

Side by side in front of the crackling fire, she held up two fingers, signifying their title had two words.

"No fair," Cash said. "Ours had like ten."

Wren landed a playful smack to his head. "What's wrong with you? Last I checked, *When Harry Met Sally* has four words and for the record, you're just a lousy actor."

"But I'm so good-looking," Cash explained, "all I have to do is stand there for everyone to be entertained."

"Aw…" Wren cupped his cheeks, drawing him in for a kiss. "I love you."

"Mmm…" Cash tugged his wife onto his lap, deepening their show of affection to a degree that made Natalie uncomfortable.

Tossing their title card to the floor, Wyatt said to the happy couple, "Can you two get your hands off each other so we can get this stupid game over with?"

"Nice, Wyatt." Dallas cast his brother one of his legendary scowls. "Way to support a night of family fun."

"Sorry," Wyatt mumbled, "I still have a lot of packing to do. Lists to double-check."

Natalie knew Wyatt's statement to be true, but it still stung knowing he'd rather be anywhere than with her. Irrationally, she felt as if she'd been transported back in time to when Craig had walked out her door. He'd been busy, too. Far too busy even to share raising his own child.

A knot blocking her throat, Natalie managed, "I—I need to use the restroom."

"Now look what you did," Dallas said to his younger brother. "Nat, he didn't mean it. Come back."

Too late. She'd already locked the door.

"Go after her," Josie urged, her voice muffled.

"Why?" Wyatt asked. "It's not my fault she's a hormonal mess."

Hands covering her face, Natalie sat on the closed toilet, taking a tissue from a nearby dispenser to blow her nose.

This was supposed to have been a pleasant, relaxing holiday. Her parents had wanted her to spend it in Chicago with them and some distant relatives, but because Josie had whined, Natalie had succumbed. Of course, the opportunity to avoid her parents had made her decision somewhat easier. Now, she recognized it for the mess it was.

No matter how much she'd been trying to avoid the fact that she was soon to be a single mom, the time until her delivery barreled toward her.

A knock sounded on the bathroom door. "Nat? Please let me in."

Josie. Natalie knew her friend was worried about her spending too much time alone, but why couldn't she see that as bad as Craig had hurt her, and now, Wyatt, she honestly preferred being alone?

Natalie forced a deep, fortifying breath, then let her supposed friend into her hideout.

"Sweetie, I'm sorry," Josie said, wrapping Natalie in a hug. "I really thought a little family fun would be just the thing to make you smile. Now, I see I might have been better off serving you thirds of dessert."

"You think?" Natalie asked with a sniffle. "Craig didn't want me and now Wyatt can't even stand being around me long enough to play a game. Do you have any idea how mortifying that is?"

"Stop. He's busy. His grumpy mood has nothing to do with you. As for Craig…" Josie swept hair from in front of Natalie's eyes, tucking it behind her ear. "You're gorgeous, and Craig's running away has way more to do with his character—or lack thereof—than yours."

Natalie appreciated Josie's stab at comfort, but unfortunately, the damage to her heart had already been done.

The Monday after Thanksgiving, seated in the backseat of her parents' minivan, Natalie felt more as though she were twelve on the way home from school than having picked up her parents from Tulsa International.

"When you told us you were pregnant," her mother, Opal, said, "I assumed you and Craig would get back together."

"I did, too," Natalie admitted, closing her eyes to ward off car sickness as the van took another turn. "I truly believed Craig and I were getting married. When he left…"

Her mother reached around her seat for a sympathetic knee pat. "Don't you worry. We'll find you a man right away."

"I've already told you," Natalie said, "I plan on raising this baby on my own."

Her father, Bud, snorted. "Think again, little lady. By my calculations, you're running out of time to give this baby a proper last name."

"I have to agree," her mom said with an exaggerated nod. "Weed Gulch is a small town. I know unwed women have babies all the time, but not in our family." Rummaging in her purse, then pulling out a tissue, Opal dabbed the corners of her eyes before blowing her nose. "My friend Alice has a boy who just got back from Iraq. He's an excellent provider and she says he has aspirations to own his own ranch. I'll call to set up a date."

Hand to her forehead, Natalie said, "Stop. You both sound crazy. I'm a self-sufficient, strong woman. Why do you think I need a man to have this baby?"

Opal didn't just remain misty, but started to wail.

One hand on the wheel, Bud used his other to stroke his wife's hair.

Natalie sighed. "I'm sorry your daughter and grandchild are such a disappointment."

"Don't you dare cop an attitude," Opal said past sniffles. "I'm sorry. No matter what, I'll always be proud of you. I'm also sad. I want more for you. Daddy and I have been married for over thirty years. We've shared everything—especially raising you. It's not that I think you can't handle raising a child on your own, I'm just sad you feel you have to."

"Mom—did you even listen when I told you Craig left me? I was devastated. Truthfully, I wanted to marry him so badly I'd stopped insisting we use birth control. I stupidly believed a baby would be the answer to all my prayers, but I was wrong. Now I'm hurt and confused and angry. I understand him not wanting me, but how could Craig reject our child?"

"I'M SORRY." IN THE teacher's lounge Tuesday morning, Josie covered Natalie's hand. "What is it with the old guard of this town believing a woman can't—or shouldn't—raise a child on her own? This is the same kind of thing Georgina pulled with Dallas and me. I never pegged Opal and Bud to be so judgmental."

Nodding, Natalie forced down a bite of her peanut butter and honey sandwich. "They tried cloaking their condemnation with concern. I knew better. Their expressions weren't all that different from when I got caught with beer on prom night."

"Wasn't Wyatt nabbed in that massive bust, too?" Josie finished her egg salad.

Natalie snorted. "I'd forgotten my brief satisfaction when Principal Ving shone his flashlight smack between Wyatt's beady eyes."

"He doesn't have beady eyes." Munching a dill pickle, Josie said, "Point of fact, they're a delicious shade of fudge-brown."

"Whatever." Natalie focused on the walnut brownie she'd brought for dessert. All right, so even back in high school Natalie had found Wyatt's gaze mesmerizing. That didn't make her any less put out with him for his attitude at their last few meetings. On a positive note, he'd soon be gone for a nice, long time.

"So what's your plan for handling your parents?"

"There's nothing much I can do." Handing Josie her second pint-size carton of milk to open, she added,

"Unless you consider a marriage of convenience to be a viable option. In which case, I'll hire a husband—but it'll have to be on credit, as what little cash I have is earmarked for the baby."

"You know Dallas and I will help any way we can. From clothes to a crib to diapers, you name it and it's yours." Josie, being a kindergarten teacher, was a master at opening milk. Unfortunately, she'd been so busy with her task that she'd missed Natalie's sour expression. "Here you go."

"Thanks."

"Playing devil's advocate," Josie said, "let's say you were able to find a man who wanted nothing more than to love you and be a father to your child. Are you saying you wouldn't marry him?"

"I'm not saying that. And I'm more than a little miffed you'd even suggest it. But read my lips—men are scum." Natalie wadded the remains of her lunch into a ball of brown paper bag and plastic wrap. Standing, she pitched her trash in the bin alongside the microwave stand. "See you later for bus duty."

"Aw, Nat…" Josie went to her, ambushing her in another hug. "I'm sorry. Don't be mad. The thing is, now that I have kids, I know how impossible it would be for me to raise them without Dallas's help."

"That's you. Like I told my folks, Craig destroyed what little remained of my heart. I was a fool to believe I could change him. Even more of a fool to try. Maybe I'm just as delusional to believe I can raise this baby on my own?"

"Calm down," Josie urged when Natalie was finally getting to the core of the matter. Was she capable of endless rounds of early morning feedings and furniture assembly and deciphering every little noise the baby made? "We still have plenty of time to figure things out. And if by your third trimester you happen to meet Prince Charming, I'll help with that, too."

Palms pressed to the wood door, Natalie pushed it open, welcoming the hall's cooler air.

"Nat, wait," Josie pleaded.

The professional counselor in Natalie knew she shouldn't be among students until regaining control of her emotions, but at the moment the sad, scared, exhausted pregnant woman she'd become lacked the energy to care.

Why did everyone in her life seem to think all she had to do was hook up with a guy and her every worry would vanish at the end of a rainbow-crowned unicorn trail? Why couldn't they understand that while the mere thought of raising her child alone could send her racing to the bathroom with another bout of nausea, the prospect of losing herself in another dead-end relationship hurt even more.

THREE DAYS.

That was all the time Wyatt had remaining until he could get the hell out of town. If he possessed one lick of smarts, he'd have hopped an early flight out of Tulsa bound for a sunny interim beach. As it was, in anticipation of an upcoming winter storm, he battled the crowds in Reasor's grocery, stocking up on enough toilet paper, milk, Doritos and beer to get him through the next few days.

Used to be, he would've used a snowstorm as an opportunity for an extended sleepover at the home of his most current blonde. After all, if he had to be stuck inside, riding out a storm, he might as well have someone cuddly on hand to keep him warm.

Maybe he was getting too old for short-term hook-ups, or maybe he had a case of boredom, but try as he might Wyatt hadn't made a single call to secure a storm *buddy.* Truth was, he was antsy to get started on this new chapter of his life and until then, he wanted to be left alone.

He'd just snagged the sole box of Froot Loops when the last person he cared to see careened onto the cereal aisle. Not in the mood for Natalie, Wyatt held his ground, doing nothing to acknowledge her other than tip his hat.

In that snippy, Miss Priss voice of hers she noted, "You are aware your mom and Josie have already stocked enough food at the ranch to survive two winter storms?"

"Last I checked, they haven't done squat to fill my pantry." Whether from windchill or fighting the crowd, the heightened color in Natalie's cheeks looked good on her.

"Why stay at your house when your whole family plans on holing up in the main house?"

On that, he had to chuckle. "Um, let's just say that fact alone is all I needed to convince me to ride this one out on my own. Ask me, I've got too many nieces. The whole damned ranch is overrun with women."

She laughed. "Your brothers seem to think that's a good thing. What about Cash and Luke? Why not use this storm as an opportunity to spend more time with them?"

Wyatt crammed his hands into his jeans pockets. Good Lord, the woman loved to bicker. "You should've been a lawyer."

"Why's that?"

"'Cause you argue damn near every point I make."

"Excuse me." A wild-haired brunette with a screaming baby hitching a ride in the shopping cart and two whiny toddlers in tow wedged between Wyatt and Natalie, snatching up sugary cereal as if each box were a gold bar.

"Poor woman," Natalie noted once she'd left. "Having three that close in age must be rough."

Wyatt snorted. "Apparently her man's never heard of condoms."

Only when Natalie's expression shifted from her usual pinched know-it-all mode to openmouthed shock, and a teary-eyed melancholy that included cupping her hands protectively to her baby bump, did Wyatt realize how his words must've stung. Had that been the case with Natalie's boyfriend, Craig? One wild night with no protection and *bam*—she'd been knocked up?

At one time, if Wyatt had found himself with a woman in Natalie's condition, he'd have married her on the spot. Lately, he'd come to realize he was lucky to not have a future full of kids. Munchkins were loud and sticky and way more trouble than their apparent worth.

"Wyatt Buckhorn," Natalie said as if his name were a dirty word, "I hope you lose power and freeze up in that modern monstrosity of a house. But then wait— how could a little cold weather bother you when you already have ice running through your veins? Your family loves you, yet you're too thickheaded to recognize just how much. Ever think of the obvious by telling them the truth behind why you're leaving?"

In a low tone he fired back, "Ever think of keeping my private matters private?"

"Sorry." Crossing her arms, she raised her chin. "I

just thought it might be nice for the twins to spend a little more time with their uncle."

"That might be, but did it ever occur to you I don't feel capable of spending my last few days here with them? In case you missed the memo, I want nothing more than to lock myself in a kid-free zone—which, considering the ever-growing size of your belly, now includes you."

HAD SHE BEEN A CAT, NATALIE could've purred with contentment. Wyatt's forked tongue trapped at the ranch, her groceries put up, the scent of beef stew filling her home with its mouthwatering promise of a hearty meal, a fire crackling in the hearth and a stack of her favorite horror DVDs ready to watch—she was more than ready to ride out what forecasters were now calling a historic blizzard in high style.

In front of the sofa, she'd set up the card table, and while the opening credits to *The Shining* rolled, she assembled her scrapbooking materials, determined to finish her mother's Christmas gift even though Natalie was currently more than a little frustrated with Opal.

By the time the movie ended, freezing rain had turned to blowing snow. Flakes fell so thick and fast Natalie couldn't see her neighbor's home across the street.

She added a log to the fire then went to the kitchen to check on the stew.

The wind blew so hard the fifty-year-old house shuddered.

Josie had invited her to stay at the ranch. There was more than enough room for Natalie to have had her own wing, but lately she'd begun feeling like a third wheel around her friend and doting husband. For all of her harsh words to Wyatt, now that she'd calmed down, she wholly understood his reasons for steering clear of his family. Dallas and Josie. Cash and Wren. Daisy and Luke. So many babies. So many happy endings. The Buckhorns were disgustingly happy and fertile. A pheromone-meter would no doubt spike off the chart!

With a bowl of stew and crackers in hand, Natalie returned to the living room. Time to really amp up the destruction with *Alien.*

On the TV, part of *Nostromo*'s crew crept through alien pods. The scene never failed to thoroughly freak out Natalie. It reminded her of the time Wyatt and a few of his friends had brought snake eggs to school and they'd hatched in the girls' locker room. Not cool.

Rapping on the front door jolted her from the unpleasant memory. Who in their right mind would be out on a night like this?

She flipped on the porch light and peered out the window.

Only the window was useless, covered in ice.

Upon opening the front door, the icy wind's slap was nothing compared to the shock of seeing Wyatt. His long, wheat-colored duster and cowboy hat were coated with snow. The way he towered over her made him seem like a snowy beast. His dark expression did nothing to help dispel her negative impression.

"What are you doing? Get inside." She yanked him by his coat sleeve into the warmth of her home. Though this was the last place she'd ever want him to be, in this weather she'd have offered the same kindness to a side-of-the-road drifter. "Take your snowy things off and stand by the fire."

"Wish I could." He at least took off his hat. His dark hair held the shape and curled against his neck. She ignored her crazy urge to touch it. "Look, there's no easy way to say this, so I'm just going to blurt it out."

Her stomach clenched. "Uh, okay."

"My brother and Josie were hit by a tractor-trailer rig. It looks bad. They were—"

"How bad are we talking?" she asked, her voice sounding distant to her own ears. She couldn't lose her best friend. She refused. "They're all right? Please, tell me they're going to be fine."

Lips pressed tight, he took a deep breath and slowly exhaled.

"Answer me, damn it." In full panic mode, she pushed his chest.

He captured her wrists, drawing her against him and holding tight. "I'd give anything to tell you what you want to hear, but last I heard, they're both pretty banged up. Highway patrol had them airlifted to Saint Francis in Tulsa. They were lucky to have a window through the storm."

"What were they doing out by the highway? From school, Josie told me they were going straight home."

"Don't know," Wyatt said, still holding strong.

"The twins? And Mabel and Esther?"

"All fine at the house. But that's why I'm here. Daisy and Luke took Mom to Tulsa. Wren was called in to work the E.R., so Cash drove her. That leaves me and you to look after the entire Buckhorn brood."

"*All* of them?"

He nodded. "Kolt's the only one with them now, so we need to hustle. Pack a bag. Judging by this weather, we may be stuck together for a good, long while."

WHILE NATALIE GRABBED clothes and toiletries, Wyatt got her house ready for the storm. He opened the cabinets beneath her bathroom and kitchen sinks, leaving a trickle of water running to protect her pipes from freezing. He dowsed the fire in her hearth and unplugged any electronics that might be hurt by power outages and then the surges that sometimes hit when the current came back on.

All the while, he prayed.

As much as Dallas drove Wyatt crazy, as the eldest brother, he'd assumed their father's role. Yes, if needed, Wyatt could assume those duties, but selfishly, he didn't want to. Dallas had worked hard to achieve his perfect life and he sure as hell didn't deserve for it to be snatched away from him prematurely. Worse yet, what if Dallas made it okay, only to have Josie die? For Dallas to lose two wives would be more than any man could bear. The twins losing their second mother was inconceivable.

"I'm ready." Natalie stood in the shadowy hall, her face blotchy from tears. She held a yellow suitcase that looked like a flower bouquet had exploded across it. Under normal circumstances, Wyatt might've given her hell for the ugly thing, but at the moment, he just held out his hand to take it.

"Oh—" Turning to the kitchen, she said, "I left stew on the stove."

"Already packed it to go and washed the pan."

Eyes wide, she put her hand to her forehead. "Is this really happening?"

"Me washing dishes?" He forced a smile. "Do it all the time."

"I'm not kidding, Wyatt. Josie's like a sister to me."

"News flash—Dallas *is* my brother. Trust me, I'm just as concerned as you. But if we lose our cool, where does that leave the kids who are now in our care?"

She averted her gaze. "You're right. Let's go."

Slapping his hat on his head and boots on his feet, Wyatt followed her out the door. Odds were his brother and sister-in-law would be fine. Wyatt was the real one in trouble. How was he supposed to survive the night with not only uptight Natalie, but all those screaming kids?

Outside, horizontal snow pelted Wyatt's cheeks. The cold was brutal enough to burn his lungs.

Once Natalie managed to lock the door, Wyatt helped her through the already drifting snow. He'd left the truck running, with the headlights on—a good thing, considering visibility was near zero. He opened her door, helped her inside, then tossed her suitcase on the backseat of the extended cab.

Behind the wheel, the truck's warmth came as a relief. There was still comfort to be found in a world gone eerily white.

"This is crazy," Natalie said, warming her hands in front of blowing heat vents. "Why were Josie and Dallas out in this?"

"Wish I knew." With the truck already in four-wheel drive, Wyatt eased away from the curve, flashing the lights to bright. It didn't do much to help him see ten feet in front of the bumper.

Natalie took her phone out, only to tuck it back in her purse. "No service. I need to know what's going on."

"Check mine." Wyatt fished it from his back pocket, tossing it to her.

"Nope."

Inches slowly turned to miles. Making a left onto the county road leading to the ranch, he glanced Natalie's way to find her crying. In the lights from the dash tears glistened on her cheeks.

"They're going to be fine."

"How do you know? How do you even know we're going to safely make it to your mom's?"

Having not seen another vehicle on the road since they'd started, Wyatt felt reasonably safe stopping in the center of the road. Angling to face her, he said, "To be honest, at the moment, I'm not sure how the truck's even staying on the road. The one thing I am sure of is how much Josie and Dallas love each other and their kids. It's going to take a hell of a lot more than bad weather or even a barreling semi to keep all of them apart."

Tears still falling, Natalie nodded, but Wyatt could tell she was still consumed by fear.

What he didn't want her to know was that he was, too. If Dallas died...

Wyatt honestly didn't know what he'd do.

Chapter Five

"Thanks for the update," Natalie said two hours later to Georgina on the ranch's landline. The drive over had been harrowing. Bless Kolt's heart, in the forty-five minutes it'd taken to make what was typically a fifteen minute drive, he'd kept all of the girls comfy and warm and watching *Cinderella.* Alas, Natalie knew she and Wyatt were living on borrowed time until the gang realized it'd be a while before their parents got home. "Please call again the second you hear anything new."

"How are they?" Wyatt asked from a kitchen table chair.

Natalie joined him at the table. "Want the good news or bad?"

"Bad."

Josie and Dallas's injury list was so extensive Natalie had taken notes, which she now consulted. "Y-your brother is unconscious, his right leg is shattered and there were so many other relatively minor issues I lost track." Swallowing past a hard knot of tears, she continued, "J-Josie is also unconscious with head trauma and a fractured pelvis."

Wyatt groaned. "The good?"

Past a tear-framed exaggerated grin, Natalie said,

"They're both barely alive, but if they survive the night, they should recover within weeks—but possibly months."

"Months?" He leaned forward, thumping his head to the table. "Where does that leave us? After this snow, you've got school. I leave town in three days."

"I can't speak for you, but as Esther's godmother, I plan to do what I promised and watch over her for however long it takes."

"Yeah, but what about the six other kids?" He didn't bother raising his head. "I have a work visa that was no easy task to get. An entire crew is depending on me."

"Well…" Natalie sighed. "For now, let's just make it through the storm. After that, no doubt Josie and Dallas will be much improved and roads will be cleared just in time for you to catch your flight." Nudging his shoulder, she added, "Chin up. It'll be fun. We'll make popcorn and roast marshmallows. Time will fly by."

"UNCLE WYATT," BONNIE SAID as Callie and Esther screamed their fool heads off, "you're a superbad babysitter."

"Thanks," he grumbled. The movie hadn't even finished and already all hell was breaking loose. While Natalie searched for diapers, Wyatt had been assigned feeding duty. Only he didn't have a clue what kids this small were even supposed to eat. Horrible with dates, Wyatt figured Callie, Daisy and Luke's second child, had to be nearly one.

"Esther only drinks Mommy's milk," Betsy announced. "Like from her boobs."

Was it wrong for Wyatt to feel a bit faint? Hands bracketing his mouth, he shouted, "Nat!"

"And see how she's drooping?" Bonnie noted.

"You're not supposed to put her in the high chair 'cause her neck doesn't got muscles."

"I want cookie!" From her booster seat, Mabel's wail struck Wyatt square between his eyes. She was Dallas and Josie's first child together. Wyatt supposed Mabel fell square in the toddler category—old enough to carry out basic skills, but none that truly matter. As if crying weren't enough, she added kicking her feet and hitting the table with chubby palms. "I want cookie!"

Robin, Cash and Wren's daughter who had to be almost three, sat in her booster seat, perfectly calm, but scribbling with a crayon on the oak table.

"What's wrong?" Natalie said, out of breath from running down the back stairs. "Did one of the kids get hurt?"

Kolt looked up from his handheld video game. "Uncle Wyatt almost killed Esther."

"Did not," Wyatt said, taking instant oatmeal from the pantry.

"We're having that for dinner?" Betsy asked. "Gross. I'm calling Mommy and Daddy."

"You can't," Wyatt snapped.

"Come here, little one." Voice cotton-soft, Natalie scooped Esther from the high chair, showing off by expertly supporting the infant's head. "That's it," she said with a light jiggle. "Shhh… I'm pretty sure your mom left you some milk in the fridge."

Wyatt asked Natalie, "How did I not get the memo Josie was breast-feeding?"

"My mom did with Callie, too." Kolt paused his game. "Dad says it's healthier for the baby and helps them not get ear infections and stuff. But when Callie started biting real bad, Mom quit. Now, she eats whatever we have for dinner—just mashed up." Taking his sister from her chair, he jiggled her much the same way Natalie handled his cousin. "You really are kinda bad at this, Uncle Wyatt. What're you going to do when you have kids?"

Knowing Kolt meant his question in a perfectly innocent way did little to ease Wyatt's pain. Hands up in the universal sign of surrender, Wyatt said, "Sorry, folks, but I need a breather."

"What's that?" Bonnie asked. She'd taken a tub of chocolate ice cream from the freezer and was now stabbing it with a spatula.

"He's gotta breathe." Betsy ate strawberry ice cream with a fork. "Like that Brad kid at school who has *acksma.*"

"Asthma," Natalie corrected. "And I don't think your uncle has that particular affliction."

"I want cookie!" Mabel kicked the table so hard her booster seat nearly fell off its chair.

"Better give her one," Bonnie said. "She bites."

"Cookie! Cookie! Mommy! Cookie!"

"I know you need your *breather,*" Natalie said under her breath, passing Esther to Wyatt, "but at the moment, we have more pressing needs."

Unbuckling Mabel's safety belt, Natalie held her, humming a cheery tune while drying the still-huffing child's tears with a paper towel. "There you go, angel. All better. Once we have dinner, we'll have cookies for dessert."

"I'm having mine now." Bonnie dredged an Oreo through her ice cream.

"No, you're not." Natalie took the ice cream and cookie.

"Oooh," Betsy said, "that wasn't very nice. Bonnie's gonna be mad at you."

"Yes, I am!" Bonnie chased Natalie to the trash can, but was too late to save her treat. "Betsy, what's Daddy's phone number? I'm telling!"

Having long since put his sister Callie on the floor, Kolt rolled his eyes.

Wyatt jiggled Esther, but she grew more fitful. "Kolt, help me out. What am I doing wrong?"

Bonnie said, "She doesn't like you, Uncle Wyatt. Me, neither."

"Wyatt?" Natalie called from the sink, where she used a wet rag to wipe down Betsy's ice cream–coated face. "Did you bring in my stew from the truck?"

"No," he said, "but I will."

Natalie had put Mabel on the floor, where she proceeded to grab fistfuls of dry dog food from a stainless steel bowl.

"Honey, no!" Natalie scooped Mabel up, only to pass her off to Kolt. "Hold her while the twins and I find Prissy."

"Okay, whoa." With a shake of his head, Wyatt said, "Seven kids *and* Wren's high-maintenance pooch?"

"And Kitty!" Betsy said, reminding them to watch out for Josie's cat.

"Poke a fork in me," Wyatt said. "I'm done."

"Congratulations." Natalie's tone was as lackluster as her expression. "We've been parents all of an hour and already you're throwing in the towel?"

Esther began to cry.

As did Callie.

And Robin.

Betsy and Bonnie clamped their hands over their ears.

"Prissy!" Mabel squirmed free from Kolt, charging as only a toddler can across the kitchen and midway up the back staircase.

The spoiled-rotten Yorkie/Chihuahua mix took one look at the drooling, pinching menace headed her way and ran off yelping.

At which point, Mabel plopped her behind on a stair and joined her cousins' wailing.

"Ohmygosh," Natalie said in a rush. Her complexion had grown red and splotchy and the way she stood with her hands on her ever-growing belly made Wyatt wonder if she was having second thoughts about becoming a mom. Forcing deep breaths, she now waved her hands in front of her face. "I'm a school counselor. I'm with kids every day. Granted, not kids this little, but I'm thinking we have to be going about this wrong. What are we missing?"

Bonnie raised her hand.

Wyatt asked, "What do you need, squirt?"

"I was just gonna say if you feed us all ice cream for dinner then the babies won't cry."

Sighing, Wyatt said, "Sounds like a plan to me."

"No deal," Natalie said above the tears. "That's like rewarding them for poor behavior."

"They're just babies," Kolt pointed out. "They don't even know what's going on." He took a bag of corn chips from the pantry. "And you guys still haven't told us where all the other grown-ups are."

Natalie held Esther and Callie.

Kolt sat on the stairs alongside Mabel and Robin, coaxing smiles from them with chips.

The sudden silence—save for blizzard-strength winds—struck Wyatt as deafening. It also brought the same brand of quivery relief as the calm after being violently ill. Like he'd survived, but now what?

"Where's my dad and mom?" Bonnie asked.

Natalie put the children down and sat on the center of one of the lower steps, patting the empty spaces alongside her. "Come here. What I have to tell you might sound scary, but I *promise,* everything's going to be fine."

TWO HOURS LATER, WYATT SAID, "That was really messed up."

"What?" The younger kids were in bed, the three oldest playing Monopoly. Natalie scrubbed Georgina's kitchen. Dinner had been a full-on catastrophe. Wyatt sat at the table, bare feet resting on the chair opposite his. He wore faded jeans and a black T-shirt a size too small from what Natalie guessed had been too many washings. The way it hugged his chest ought to be criminal. It showcased far too many of his muscular assets. Not a good thing, considering she was stuck with him at least until the end of the storm. The only help he'd given at dinner was to second guess her every decision. "You going to tell me I'm as lousy at dish-washing as I am cooking?"

"Point of fact," he said, nursing a longneck beer, "your stew hit the spot. My problem is more in the way of how you promised the girls their parents were going to be fine."

"They are." Natalie refused to think any other way.

Feet planted on the floor, he leaned forward with his palms on the table. "Both Dallas and Josie have more wrong than right. What are you going to tell the twins if their parents' recovery doesn't go as planned?"

"Are you purposely trying to make this situation

worse than it already is?" Natalie abandoned the dishes to face him. "Like it or not, the two of us are the only thing standing between a bunch of kids and the worst winter storm this state has seen in years—if not ever. Trust me, I'm not any happier than you about being stuck here together. If I had my druthers, I'd put you on a plane this second."

He finished his beer. "You don't mean that."

"The hell I don't." No matter how badly her throat ached from the effort of holding back tears, she wasn't about to let him see her cry for a second time in one day. His every word reinforced her vow to stay single. She'd forgotten a man's capacity to hurt. "Every chance you get, you tear me down. Why? What have I ever done to deserve you treating me like scum you wiped off your boots?"

"Now you're being—" Before he could finish his sentence, a low descending hum signaled the house powering down. "Swell."

"I'll find candles," Natalie said.

"Where are the lights?" Betsy asked, Bonnie close on her heels.

"I told her," Kolt said, "the electricity went out because of the snow, but she's too dumb to listen."

"Don't call your cousin dumb." Natalie sensed Wyatt behind her. His size, the chemistry that crackled between them was unnerving. Her brain knew she'd had enough of Wyatt, but her body didn't get the memo.

"Excuse me," she said to him, fumbling through a drawer where she'd seen matches.

For an instant, his hand touched hers. "Sorry."

Did he feel it, too? The heat, tightening his stomach whenever she was near? Natalie prayed she wasn't the only one being tortured.

"Found them." Thrilled for the distraction, Natalie struck a match against the box. Her eyes fought the flame's glow. "Betsy, Bonnie, could you please help me find the cupboard where your grandmother keeps her candles?"

"This will work better." Wyatt brandished a flashlight, waving the beam in her face.

"Until the batteries go dead." The match burned down to her fingers, scorching in the second before she'd blown it out. Acting on instinct, she lifted her stinging finger to her mouth, licking where it most hurt. In the process, her gaze met Wyatt's. Her mind's eye had him kissing not only her finger, but so much more. Which was wrong and disturbing in ways she didn't dare explore.

Bonnie held up her treasure. "Here's some candles, Miss Natalie, but Grandma only lets people use them on special days."

"I got some, too," Betsy said.

"Thanks." Natalie took the girls' offerings, but still headed to the dining room not only for holders, but to escape Wyatt. The house was enormous. Why did his presence have it feeling cramped all of the sudden?

Without the electrical hum of appliances and central heat, the wind's howl took on a frightening tone.

"I'm scared." Betsy hugged Natalie's waist.

Bonnie followed suit.

"Tell you what," Wyatt knelt in front of them, "if you ladies light candles, Kolt and I will make a big fire. Then, we'll roast marshmallows and tell ghost stories just like we did on your Halloween hayride."

"I want princess stories." Betsy frowned at the deep, dancing shadows the candlelight formed.

"Princesses are dumb." Kolt turned to Wyatt. "Come on, let's get wood."

Natalie asked, "How long until it gets cold upstairs? Think we should take the babies from the nursery?"

"Check on them," Wyatt said, "but the house is well-insulated. They've got plenty of blankets, so they should be fine till morning. If the power's still off by then, we'll make pallets nearer the fire."

She nodded.

The more candles Natalie lit, the more the home looked pretty as opposed to spooky. Beyond the great room's towering windows, the storm blew. But inside, all was calm. Except for her runaway pulse. How much longer was she destined to be stranded with Wyatt?

ALONG WITH MORNING, FOR WYATT, came the realization that not only was it still snowing, but the power was still out and his back hurt like hell from crashing on the floor while the Terror Twins were snug on the couch. Even worse, Kitty had camped out on his chest and Natalie looked seriously hot with sleep-mussed hair, cradling snoring Prissy in her arms.

Blaming the observation on cabin fever, he rolled away from her only to face Kolt.

"Let's have a snowball fight," the kid suggested, seemingly oblivious to the fact that they'd had about two hours' rest.

Wyatt groaned. "Love to, kid, but with the power still out, we've got man chores."

"Like what?" Kolt wriggled from his sleeping bag with his video game in hand. Had he held it through the night like a preteen teddy bear? "Because after we have a snowball fight, we can build a fort. Then we can fight in the fort. It's gonna be awesome!"

"Slow down." Edging upright, Wyatt eyed Natalie, who'd taken the other couch. She'd offered it to him, but what kind of jackass would he be to have made a pregnant woman sleep on the floor? "We've got to build up the fire, then check the horses and other animals. We're going to need to hook the plow to the truck, so we can make it up to your house, too. Not only do we need to check your horses, but make sure no pipes froze last night."

"Stop," Natalie said in a raspy tone that did little to help Wyatt's already frustrated condition. "You're making me want to hide under the covers."

From the baby monitor she'd placed on the coffee table came fitful cries.

Natalie said, "Esther's going to be none too pleased to find she's dining on formula this morning instead of her usual fare."

"Does that mean we're out of boob milk?" Kolt looked genuinely distraught.

"Afraid so." Natalie pushed back her covers and emerged wearing comfy gray sweatpants and a matching University of Tulsa hoodie.

Kolt asked, "Can't you make her more from your boobs?"

Lips pressed tight, Wyatt had never wished more for a sudden heat wave to melt the snow, allowing for a quick escape.

"That's a great question," Natalie said, disgustingly patient for barely 7:00 a.m., "but mothers are only able to make breast milk when they have babies."

"But my mom said you have a baby inside you," Kolt persisted.

"True," she said, "but my body won't make milk until the baby is born."

"Oh." Wyatt's nephew took a few seconds to let this sink in before digging in his sleeping bag to pull out his socks. "Can we hurry with the man stuff, because I really want to play."

"Me, too." Wyatt ruffled the kid's hair, then stoked the hearth's glowing coals before adding more logs and coaxing a flame.

Natalie had gone upstairs and now descended with Esther in her arms. Even huffing from tears, his niece was a beauty. As was the woman carrying her. Wyatt didn't have to be friends with a woman to admit she possessed positive assets.

While Kolt ran off to find snow gear, Wyatt said, "I've gotta give you props for the way you handled Kolt's question."

"Thanks." Cradling the baby, Natalie's bewildered expression made him think she'd been caught off guard by his compliment. "But in my line of work, I've had some doozies. That one was pretty tame."

Sitting in front of the fire, storing up heat for his trek to the barn, Wyatt said, "I'm sorry for last night. What I said about you promising the girls Dallas and Josie are going to be all right. Guess the way things have gone for me lately, I've gotten used to expecting the worst."

"In one respect, you have good reason." Natalie nuzzled Esther's downy hair. "But as soon as this storm clears, we'll get word that Josie and Dallas are fine. Then you'll be off on your adventure. When you get back, you've got a great family and job and home. Tons of friends."

All of which Wyatt was thankful for. But it still stung that he'd never have more. Best as he could tell, the holy grail of his family—hell, the whole state—

was getting married and starting a family. Being stuck with his nieces and nephew proved he wasn't even capable of being a good father, which should've made his condition easier to bear. At the height of the previous night's screaming fiasco, he'd have been thrilled to never see another kid again. But morning had a way of washing away the strongest resolve. The brush of Esther's long lashes against her cheeks brought on that old familiar yearning for something he'd never have.

"You all right?" Natalie stood close enough for him to reach out and take the baby from her, but he didn't. Couldn't. For him, holding a child was akin to an alcoholic holding a drink. Pointless. Why, for even a moment, grow enamored with something he could never have?

Chapter Six

"How are you gonna feed your baby, Miss Natalie, when you're not very good at feeding ours?" Bonnie had always had a knack for cutting to the heart of any matter and this time was no different.

"Yeah," Betsy said.

"How about you two help?" Natalie sat on the sofa nearest the fire attempting to bottle-feed Esther while spooning pureed blueberries into Callie's clamped mouth. Mabel and Robin happily fed themselves Cheerios, but not without making a mess.

She would have never considered feeding children in the elegant Buckhorn living room, but since the temperature in the kitchen felt perilously low, there had been no other option. She had at least placed trash bags over the handwoven rug.

"I want the baby." Bonnie held out her hands, pinching her Pop-Tarts-sticky fingers.

"You're not *sanitorily*," Betsy said. "You feed Callie."

"She's gross." Bonnie made a face. "Look at her. She's like a purple monster baby."

"That's mean! I'm telling Aunt Daisy you called her baby ugly!"

"Did not! And anyway, she *is* all covered in purple stuff!"

"Ladies…" Natalie had forgotten just how *delight-ful* the twins could be. "Please, let's just get all of the little ones fed as quickly and quietly as possible."

Oh, from then on out, the twins were quiet, they just continued to torment each other by sticking out their tongues and making faces.

Finally, Esther had eaten her fill and drifted off to sleep in her blanket-topped carrier.

As for Mabel, Callie and Robin, Natalie wasn't sure how to tell when they were full. Taking an educated guess that when there was more throwing and playing with food than eating that they were done, she launched the long cleanup process.

"Girls," she said to the twins, "while I'm picking cereal off of the floor, I need you to put on your coats, then go upstairs to bring down lots of baby toys. We're going to move the furniture to make a giant playpen."

"Can we play in it, too?" Bonnie asked.

"Sure. We'll need all of the diaper supplies, too."

Betsy said, "Bonnie doesn't like the way poop diapers smell."

"Thank you." Natalie took a deep breath, vowing to keep her cool. "We won't need dirty diapers. Just the clean ones."

The back door opened and closed. "Hello?"

The twins ran over. "Uncle Cash!"

Wyatt and Kolt entered behind him.

"Hey, squirts." After removing his boots, Cash gave both girls hugs. "How are you holding up, Nat?"

"I'm good. How are Josie and Dallas?"

"Kids," Wyatt said, "how about getting on your

snow gear and making sure the horses' water isn't frozen."

"Didn't we just do that?" Kolt said.

"With it this cold," Cash said, removing his heavy coat and gloves, "we can't be too careful."

Once the big kids were out of earshot, Natalie asked, "What's going on? Are Josie and Dallas worse?"

Cash rubbed his whisker-stubbled jaw. "Let's just say there's not been as much improvement as their doctors would like. Josie's drifting in and out of consciousness and Dallas is facing possible surgery. Daisy and Luke are staying with Mom. The E.R. has been swamped, so Wren stayed, too. But we all figured Wyatt would need a hand with the animals."

Hand over her mouth, Natalie mumbled, "I'm going to be sick." She ran to the powder room, kneeling in front of the commode.

Cash started to follow, but Wyatt stopped him. "Let me handle her."

"She doesn't need *handling,* bro, but understanding."

Wyatt shot his little brother his dirtiest look. "Give me some credit."

Cash shrugged. "Just sayin'. Where's my girl?"

Wyatt nodded toward the living room where Natalie and the twins had assembled a massive playpen.

From down the hall came sounds of Natalie alternately crying and being sick. Taking pity on her, Wyatt went to the bathroom, bringing along the flashlight to erase the dark.

After running one of Georgina's designer tea towels beneath cold water, Wyatt fell to his knees beside Natalie, holding the cloth to her forehead. "I—I know you'd rather have Josie, or one of your other girlfriends in here, but I'm afraid I'm all you've got."

Trembling, she sat on her heels.

He flushed the toilet, then freshened the cloth to wipe her face. Once he'd wiped away her tears, he sat behind her, spreading his legs to draw her against his chest. Neither of them had had a good night's rest and exhaustion couldn't be good for her or her baby.

"That's it," he murmured, stroking her long hair. "You're going to be okay. So is everyone we love."

"What if they're not?" Her voice sounded small and defeated. He liked her better loud and argumentative. This crying shell wasn't his Natalie. They'd shared a connection since grade school and now, because of Esther, they always would. No matter how much they'd lately seemed to be getting on each other's nerves, he'd always carry a soft spot for her. "Cash made it sound like they were both at death's door."

Wyatt snorted. "We both know Cash is a drama queen."

She laughed, and the sound stirred something deep within him. He'd done that—given her comfort. That fact made him feel, if only for an instant, better about the crap storm fate had made of their lives.

"You going to be okay?"

She rested her head against his chest and he felt her nod. He'd been a lot of things in his day, but a knight had never been one of them. He wouldn't make an ass of himself by assuming anything had changed. He'd have comforted anyone in Natalie's situation.

THE WEED GULCH FEED STORE was never open on Sundays, but due to the snow, too much grazing land was covered for ranchers to not rely on supplemental grain.

Many pole barns in the area had collapsed, trapping stored hay bales beneath them.

The small-town grapevine had got the word out that from noon to however long there was a need, the store owners would be there to help.

Wyatt stood with Cash in the checkout line. It felt good to be out of the house and get a change of scenery—even if at the moment that only meant whitewashed concrete block walls.

"Aren't you s'posed to leave tomorrow?" Cash asked, munching on the free popcorn always on hand. The buttery scent made Wyatt's stomach growl.

"Yep." They moved ahead in the ten-deep line.

"Still going?"

"Haven't decided," he admitted. On the one hand, if he abandoned his family when they'd never needed him more, he'd be the world's biggest jerk. On the other, he needed this trip. Bad. Being charged with the full-time care of his nieces and Kolt had called Wyatt's bluff. On Thanksgiving, the Buckhorn clan had been so rowdy he'd convinced himself he was glad he couldn't have kids. Yet now, only a couple days into the job of being a temporary parent, he'd already seen glimpses of how amazing being a true father must be.

"You okay?" Cash asked. "If I didn't know better, I'd say you look hungover. But even you wouldn't have tied one on while caring for seven kids."

"Why do you say that?" Wyatt asked under his breath. "*Even me?* Like I'm some irresponsible ogre. I've taken good care of those kids."

"Whoa." Cash held up his hands. "No one said you didn't. But by your own admission, you're not exactly the family-man type. If you were, instead of chasing off to the end of the world, you'd stick around here and find yourself a good woman."

Hand to his forehead, Wyatt prayed for calm. As much as he hated to admit it, Natalie had been right. If he did come clean with everyone he loved about the fact that he might one day marry, but would never increase the size of their clan, maybe they'd once and for all stop with the not-so-subtle hints for him to settle down.

"Just saying." Cash moved up in line. "I don't know jack about oil, maybe it's giving you everything you need to keep you warm at night, but now that I have Wren and—"

"Dear Lord," Wyatt said, "don't you ever shut up?"

Cash stayed quiet just long enough for a fresh bite of popcorn. "One last thing—if you do leave tomorrow, how are you going to live with yourself? You know no matter when or where, every last one of us would be there for you. Well now, we need you a helluva lot more than that bigwig oil company you're leaving us for."

"WHAT SHOULD I DO?" Wyatt was on his second trip to town that day—this time to get Mabel cough syrup. Cash had volunteered to stay with the kids, giving Natalie a chance to grab more clothes and toiletries. Weed Gulch proper looked worn-out. Christmas decorations that'd been perfectly hung on the historic redbrick Main Street buildings after Thanksgiving had been battered by strong winds. They now hung limp and defeated alongside dirty tinsel stars. Snow had been plowed into great mounds that occupied most available parking space. With temperatures in single digits and expected to stay that way, the road was still a nearly impassable mess. "You know, about my trip. My flight to Dallas leaves at six a.m."

"What do you want to do?" Natalie asked.

"Please don't," he said with a sigh when stopped for one of the town's three traffic lights. "I don't need counseling techniques, turning my questions back on me, but the genuine advice of a friend. I know we've spent more time lately snipping at each other than truly communicating, but Nat, I do consider you the only person I can trust when it comes to…you know."

She took the full length of the light before answering. "God's honest truth—I want you to reschedule your trip. I'm freaked out enough about having my own baby, let alone caring for Josie's whole brood. When you agreed to be Esther's godfather, you promised to care for her in the event Dallas couldn't. Do you really want to be the kind of guy who reneges on a sacred vow?"

Wyatt winced. "Whew. I should've asked for only half your opinion."

Lips pursed, she shrugged. "You wanted the truth…"

"Yeah."

Just like he knew he needed to make a tough call to the friends he was supposed to meet up with in London.

"ALL I CAN SAY IS THANK goodness Georgina prefers natural gas appliances." Two days later, the temperature had climbed to the sunny forties, steadily melting the snow and making the whole world sound as if it were dripping, but the power was still out. Natalie stood at the stove making fried eggs and bacon for Wyatt and Cash, who were about to start their daily rounds of checking the animals. In the oven, biscuits were almost done.

Dallas and Josie were making such good progress that Luke was heading home to help with the ranch. Daisy and Georgina had gotten a hotel room near the hospital.

Because school had been out due to the snow, Natalie's job hadn't been an issue, but she had a feeling once classes were back in session, she'd need to have a talk with her principal about taking more time to be with Esther and Mabel.

"No kidding," Wyatt said. "Cash, how many times have we all said we need a generator for the house? Hell, the horse barn is warmer than it is in here."

At only six in the morning, all of the kids were still sleeping. The living room looked more like a bunkhouse than Georgina's usual elegant Western-themed showplace.

Cash said, "Ran into Jimmy Middleton at the feed store yesterday. He works for AEP/PSO. With any luck, we should have power in a day or two."

"That's too long," Natalie said, flipping Wyatt's eggs. She'd learned he liked them over easy with just a hint of a runny yolk. The heat from the oven and stove had warmed the kitchen to a bearable level, but stray too far from the living room fire and the rest of the house was frigid. The hot water heater was gas, but had an electronic ignition. Same with the central heat. Thank heavens the stove could be lit with a match.

Wyatt hovered behind her. "Looks good. I'm hungry." As usual, his nearness was disconcerting, but since his kindness during her meltdown, even more so. She'd expected him to act resentful about changing his travel plans, but if anything, he seemed strangely relaxed. Almost as if now that his decision had been made, he was at peace with it.

From her nest near the fire, Esther let loose with a few pitiful wails.

Natalie said, "If one of you watch the eggs, I'll get the baby."

"I'll get her." Before she could object, Wyatt was already on his way.

"What's got him in such a good mood?" she asked his brother.

"Not sure," Cash admitted, "but it's making me suspicious."

"Got a full diaper," Wyatt said, holding Esther at a safe distance.

Cash asked, "Know much about changing diapers?"

"What do you think?" Wyatt passed Esther to his little brother. "But if you take this one, I'll watch, then tackle the next."

"Sounds doable." The two men headed to the makeshift living room changing station.

Listening to the easy banter between the brothers made Natalie ache for poor Wyatt. Cash prattled on about how once Wyatt had his own kids, he'd get the hang of diaper changing in no time, the whole while, through no fault of his own, oblivious to Wyatt's private pain.

What an odd duo she and Wyatt made for godparents. She was consumed with fear over how she'd have to single-handedly care for her child, while Wyatt feared the emptiness in his life of never having a child. Two opposite sides of a coin.

When she thought of the day she would deliver her baby, Natalie's throat tightened. How sad she would be, bringing her baby home to an empty house. As a school counselor, she was all too aware of how many single moms and dads didn't do such a great job. But then there were just as many who managed to raise well-adjusted children. She planned on doing her best in regard to her son or daughter, but what if that wasn't good enough?

AFTER BREAKFAST, WYATT fed and watered the horses.

Then he took the Jeep and checked the cattle on the ranch's desolate southwest corner. The storm had hit with such ferocity, there hadn't been time to move them. They'd lost two, and coyotes had feasted on the carcasses.

He hated this side of the business. Made him thankful for his brothers so he didn't have to do it every day. Wyatt understood that death was a natural part of life and all that, but when he spent time feeding and caring for animals, then felt guilty for eating them, he realized just what a pathetic cowboy he truly was.

Taking a shovel from the back of the Jeep, he dug a shallow grave and filled it with the remains.

Give him an oil field over this any day. He enjoyed every aspect of the business, from collecting raw field data like he'd hopefully soon be doing in Ethiopia, to helping out on a pipeline crew. Though he was qualified to be the boss, he enjoyed working with his hands. Aligning pipe segments. Guiding pipes into the trench. Even using a chain saw to clear growth from pipeline right-of-ways. Some of his most fulfilling memories had been made on Alaska's North Slope.

While there were healthy, producing wells on Buckhorn land, those were old news. Wyatt preferred the thrill of the chase and claiming new ground.

In a darker mood than when he'd left the house,

Wyatt returned late in the afternoon to find Betsy and Bonnie building a fort out of what little remained of the snow.

"Uncle Wyatt," Bonnie asked, running up to him while eating a handful of snow. "Kolt said eating snow will make a baby in me like the one Miss Natalie has in her. Is that true?"

"No." Glaring at his nephew, he said, "Kolt, what's your problem? Why would you say something like that to little girls?"

"I dunno." Chin to his chest, Kolt said, "They were being dorks and saying I have a horse nose, so I wanted to tell them something stupid back."

"If eating snow doesn't give you babies, Uncle Wyatt," Betsy talked around a huge purple wad of grape-smelling bubble gum, "then what does?"

"Ask your mom."

"She's at the hospital," Bonnie said. "And when do we get to see her and Daddy? We miss them."

"Ask Miss Natalie." Wyatt sidestepped an abandoned snowman on his walk to the back door.

He should've known Bonnie wouldn't give up that easy. "She said to ask you."

"Swell…" Ignoring the kid, he headed into the house. He'd like a hot shower. To sit down with a half-dozen beers and ESPN. What he'd get was another cold, dark night crammed together with what felt like every kid in the county.

"How were the cattle?" By the light of a single candle, he hadn't seen Natalie standing at the stove.

"Lost two." Why, he couldn't have said, but he wanted to talk about his day. How long and lonely it had been and how the dead heifers took him back in time to when his 4-H calf had died of scours. "Remember when we were in eighth grade and Sammy got sick?"

"Yeah." She placed the wooden spoon she'd been using on the counter. "My friend Dawn and I brought you cookies to make you feel better and you said the sight of me made you worse."

He took a beer from the lukewarm fridge and popped the top. "Know why I was such a little pissant to you?"

Grinning over her shoulder, she said, "Because that's your natural, obnoxious state?"

"Ha ha." He downed half the bottle in a few swigs. Mellowed by exhaustion and the intimate lighting, he confessed, "Until I learned your true evil nature, I had the worst crush on you."

"Evil?" Hands on her hips, she asked, "What did I ever do to deserve a label like that?"

Finishing the beer, he set it onto the table. "What do you think? Denied me."

"You never pursued me."

"Did in the fourth grade. You used to wear this red shirt and matching bow that drove me crazy."

"Which is why that whole year you tormented me every day to the point I cried all the way home?"

"Seriously?" He grabbed another beer.

"You thought calling me *Fatty Natty* was a turn-on?"

Leaning against the counter, he winced. "Sorry. Back then, I had the social skills of a squirrel."

"Oh—" she laughed "—and you're so much better now?"

Her quirky smile, the way light from the setting sun streamed in the window over the sink, casting a net of red over her hair, all of it melded into a force field of attraction he felt just as incapable of penetrating now as he had back in fourth grade.

A wimper sounded over the baby monitor.

"If you wouldn't mind watching dinner," Natalie said, "I'll see which of our charges is unhappy."

"Sure." Shifting toward the stove, he asked, "What are we having?"

"Chicken and dumplings."

"Sounds good. I never knew you could cook."

Casting a wink over her shoulder, she called out, "Add that to the hundred and one other things you don't know about me."

Damned if he could figure out why, but the more he learned about Natalie, the more intrigued he became.

"GUESS WHAT? GUESS WHAT?" Bonnie ran into the kitchen, where Natalie was doing dishes by candle-light. The guys had offered to handle the chore, but truthfully, it was a relief having them on baby duty. She'd always adored being around kids, but riding out the storm had been akin to jumping feetfirst into the parental fire.

"What?" Natalie asked the little girl.

"Uncle Cash said we're all going to watch a movie. I haven't watched a movie in a million, trillion years."

"Me, neither," Betsy said, staking claim to her sister's exaggeration.

"How are you going to do that?" Natalie used some of the warm water she'd heated for washing to wet a dishrag, wiping down the counters.

"Uncle Luke brought his big car back from the hospital and it has a DVD player in the backseat."

"That sounds fun. Want me to make you popcorn?"

Both girls shouted their agreement.

Cash and Luke sat in the car's front seat, web surfing on their phones, while all but the youngest kids watched a Disney double feature.

"How'd we get so lucky as to rate a quiet house?" Wyatt asked, looking up from the business magazine he'd been skimming. A fire crackled and the light of a dozen candles provided barely enough light for reading.

"Bite your tongue," Natalie whispered. Callie and Esther were sleeping, but fitfully. Callie had wanted to stay with the big kids, but was so tired she hadn't been able to hold up her head. A few minutes' rocking had sent her drifting off to dreamland. "I'm praying the babies don't wake when everyone else comes in."

"I'll text Cash to tell their crew to tiptoe."

"Thanks." Natalie felt as if she should say more, but what? Their conversation that afternoon, Wyatt's admission of harboring a secret elementary-school crush had caught her off guard. It sounded silly, but the little girl still inside her was flattered. Natalie never considered telling him that by the time they'd reached middle school, she'd taken him cookies when his calf died because she'd been crushing on him.

How different would life now be had either of them been more receptive to the other's advances?

"You're quiet," Wyatt said.

"Thought you liked me best that way."

"Ouch." He played at clutching his chest. "You know, I almost asked you to the eighth grade formal. If I had, what would you have said?"

"Seriously?" She'd just lifted her mug of hot tea, but no longer trusted herself to safely hold hot liquid. "Why bring this up now?"

"Beats me." He sighed and stretched his legs out in

front of him, crossing them at the ankles. "I had too much time to think this afternoon. Finding the dead cattle reminded me how much I hate ranching. And what a fraud I feel like even living on this ranch."

"What?" Straightening, she said, "You can't mean that. You're a Buckhorn. A cowboy through and through."

"Nah. Maybe on the outside, but inside, given the chance, after my stint in Ethiopia, I'd move to Houston and see where our little oil company could really go." The weak light brought out shadows beneath his eyes. In all the years she'd known him, she'd never heard him be so frank. Had a couple of beers loosened him up? Or was it something more? It was almost as if he felt comfortable enough with her to share his innermost thoughts. But why? Because she was a counselor?

"What's stopping you," she dared ask, "from making a permanent move?"

"Family obligations so heavy they feel like an anchor."

"Know what you mean," she said without thinking. "When my parents found out I was pregnant, they expected me to marry any man who'd have me. Oh, they claimed it was because they worried I wasn't capable of raising a child on my own, but deep down, I think they don't want the shame of having an unwed mother for a daughter."

"Sorry," he said. "It never occurred to me you'd get grief from your folks about not being married, too. Everyone's constantly nagging me to conform. Be like all of the rest of my crowd who've suddenly seen the light and found love. Only problem is, I haven't. Don't think I ever will. I'm beginning to think I'm not wired for long-term emotion."

"That's sad." The finality of his declaration forged a knot in her throat. "I've always said that after Craig hurt me, I'd never give another man the chance to hurt me. But hearing you voice what I've been thinking makes me wonder if maybe I've been too hasty. Maybe four or five years down the road, my Prince Charming will come."

"Good luck with that." He looked away as if in disgust. "Have any idea what the odds are for a single mom to find a guy willing to father another man's son?"

"Are you a monster? Why would you say something like that? Especially when seconds earlier I made a heartfelt admission I should've kept to myself."

"Sorry. Maybe I am a monster. Or hell, maybe I just no longer have a heart."

Chapter Seven

Wednesday morning, power had thankfully been re-
stored, but for Natalie, the vibe between her and Wyatt
felt strained. Josie and Dallas were being moved from
ICU to regular hospital rooms, and by the end of the
week, the plan was for them to be placed in a long-term
care facility. In the meantime, Luke had taken Kolt and
his baby sister, Callie, home. Robin and Prissy were
back at their house with Cash and their regular sitter.
As Callie usually hung out with Daisy in her office, or
at the house they'd been forever renovating, she was
also staying with Robin's sitter during the day.

As for Natalie's schedule, she had an appointment
with her principal beginning right after the morning
bell.

Mabel sat on the floor in Natalie's office, playing
with a rag doll and blocks. Esther cooed in her carrier.
Natalie sifted through email and snail mail and phone
messages. She'd barely been at it ten minutes when
her boss sidestepped Mabel's toys to have a seat on the
sofa.

"I was sick to hear about Josie and Dallas," the principal said. "Have you been to see them?"

"Not yet," Natalie said. "Georgina relayed that Josie

doesn't want the girls seeing her or their father looking so scary."

"Have they at least spoken on the phone?"

"No." Natalie played with the Slinky she kept on her desk to busy little fingers. "Georgina's assured the twins their parents will be fine, but it's not hard to see the girls are growing impatient about constantly being put off."

"I don't blame them." Clearing her throat, Principal Moody said, "You, of all people, should know children are smarter than we give them credit for. The longer the girls are kept from the reality of what's happened, the more nightmares they'll concoct in their heads."

"True. But on the flip side, from what Luke and Cash have reported, Dallas and Josie are swollen and bruised to the point they're barely recognizable. What kind of image is that for their kids to forever have in their memories? Especially if Wyatt and I can provide a certain level of continuity in their care."

Principal Moody left the sofa to lift Esther from her carrier. "Seems like just yesterday we were celebrating this little one's christening."

"I know," Natalie managed to say past the knot in her throat. How could so much have changed, yet stayed the same? Her best friends nearly died. Wyatt was in her life, but back to playing a superficial role.

"I don't mean to pry, but how are you and Wyatt managing? Four kids are a lot to handle when your relationship is still young."

"O-our relationship?" Natalie shook her head.

"When I saw you and Wyatt kiss that afternoon, I assumed…"

"No." Was it possible for a human to turn twenty shades of red?

"So then he's not the father of your…" She gestured toward Natalie's growing belly.

Mouth dry, Natalie answered with a shake of her head.

"Yes, well, Cami tells me you need paperwork for a leave of absence?"

"We have no idea how long Josie and Dallas may be incapacitated, and I'd feel better watching Esther and Mabel myself than putting them in day care."

"I understand," Principal Moody said, "but we'll sorely miss you around here."

"I'll miss all of you, too."

Natalie packed a few essentials from her desk—lipstick and Oreo cookies—then put Mabel back in her stroller, balancing Esther's carrier on top.

From school, she settled her crew into their car seats for a trip to the grocery store, where Mabel pitched at least three hissy fits and Esther screamed until she couldn't breathe. Good times, followed by even more fun at the gas station and pharmacy.

Once Natalie returned to the ranch, then unloaded kids and groceries, half her day was gone.

Mabel was still cranky from not getting her way at the store, and Esther seemed hungry. After giving Mabel a juice box and graham crackers, Natalie settled into the living room's comfy rocker to feed the baby her bottle.

"You're good with her."

Natalie glanced up to see Wyatt. "I didn't hear you come in."

He shrugged, landing on a seat opposite hers. "She likes you."

"At this point, the poor thing would probably bond

with anyone who has a bottle. As cranky as she's been, I can tell she misses Josie and Dallas."

"I talked to Mom this morning." Wyatt removed his cowboy hat and ran his hand through his hair. "She said Josie and Dallas want to see the kids, but for us to wait until Saturday to bring them."

"Why so long?"

"I guess for more of their facial bruising and cuts to heal."

By way of acknowledgment, she nodded. The last time she and Wyatt had been alone, the things he'd said... Suffice to say, her already lackluster opinion of the man had only gotten worse.

The house was too quiet.

The grandfather clock ticked too loud.

Wyatt cleared his throat. "I've been with enough women to know I'm getting the silent treatment."

Just what every girl wanted to hear. Glancing his way, she shook her head.

"If you're still ticked about movie night—sorry." Leaning forward, he braced his elbows on his knees. "Lately, I feel dark inside. Like the happier everyone I love becomes, the more miserable I am."

"News flash—your brother and sister-in-law aren't exactly whooping it up."

"You know what I mean." He stood and paced like a penned bull. "Before all of this, I'd never really considered who would miss me if I hid out in Ethiopia for a few years, or for that matter, died, but their accident has me facing my own mortality."

Natalie repositioned Esther, who was taking her sweet time finishing her bottle. "You do realize every word out of your mouth contradicts your last tantrum?"

"Um, no." Narrowed eyes told her he was upset she'd even suggest such a thing.

"Which is it? Are you a monster with no heart? Or a mere mortal with a heart so huge it feels empty without a family of your own to share it?"

He froze, staring at her with a mix of anger and maybe realization.

Mabel had been at the coffee table, coloring princesses with chunky crayons. She now stood toe-to-toe with Wyatt's boots, holding up her arms, wiggling her fingers and grinning. "Airplane!"

While Wyatt just stood there, looking at the child as if she'd sprouted pointy alien ears, Mabel added hopping to her adorable routine.

"Airplane! Airplane!"

He knew full well what the toddler wanted. Dallas regularly swooped her up, flying her around while making silly *vroom* noises. What was wrong with Wyatt that he couldn't do the same?

After ruffling the girl's hair, he said, "I've gotta make a few calls. I'll be back in time to occupy the twins while you fix dinner."

Mabel toddled after him, but soon gave up, falling onto her bottom in a fit of outraged tears.

Esther had drifted off to sleep, so Natalie placed her in her carrier and picked up Mabel, doing her best to replicate Dallas's game. Soon enough, the girl giggled, but she was heavy and Natalie's arms couldn't bear the weight.

Breathless, she collapsed on the sofa, snuggling Mabel alongside her. "Your uncle Wyatt is crazy."

The girl nodded. "Cra-zie."

"What are we going to do about it?"

"Cookies!" Mabel laughed.

The little girl's enthusiasm was catching. It made Natalie look forward to the day when she played with her own son or daughter. Instead of being terrified of her looming deadline, she needed to start looking forward to her baby's birth.

"Know what?" Natalie said with a tweak of the girl's nose, "I think you're right. Cookies are exactly what this situation needs."

"WE EVER GOING TO SEE YOU?" Cale Montrose, one of the guys Wyatt was supposed to have met in London for the trek down to Africa, sounded staticky on his satellite phone. "We're poised to make the biggest find of the decade. Thought you wanted in?"

"I do…" Running his palm over his stubbled jaw, Wyatt sighed. "Things are complicated over here. But give me a month—two, tops—and I'll grab the first flight over."

"That long?" The bad connection didn't hide disappointment in Cale's tone. "We need you, man."

"I know, and I'm sorry. Really, I am, but—"

"Look," Cale said, "I feel for your family and all, but if you're not over here in say, two weeks, we're going to have to find a replacement. Our crew's too streamlined to head out into the backcountry without a rock hound. *Capisce?*"

"Yeah." After a few minutes' small talk, Wyatt hung up. Swell. Just freakin' swell. He'd spent the last year putting this trip together. From getting his Ethiopian visa to making sure everything here on the home front ran like a Buckhorn-oiled machine. In the Tulsa office were folks who inspected and maintained current wells they owned, and looked into obtaining ones they should. All the way in Alaska were more wells and a pipeline in need of maintenance. It took everything in him to juggle it all. The fact that he'd finally nailed down the details to the point that he could now juggle with no hands brought on mixed feelings. Part of him obviously couldn't wait to get the hell out of Weed Gulch. Another part—one he'd never admit having— was a little hurt that he'd been so easily replaced.

Assuming he did get his chance to wing off to Africa, what then? Would his family, friends, coworkers even notice he was gone? If not, that stung. It also spoke volumes about the kind of bitter, cold creep he'd become.

When Mabel had wanted to play airplane, why hadn't he just gone ahead and picked her up? Just because he couldn't have his own children, did that make him incapable of showing kindness to his brothers'? How many years had Wyatt told himself he was content with a constant string of blondes, but maybe he did want more. Only what was the point in wanting something impossible to obtain?

Nearly losing Dallas had shaken Wyatt to his core.

It'd made him realize he couldn't forever run from his inability to father kids. Sooner or later, he needed to tell his brothers and sister. Maybe then he'd at least find peace in sharing their babies?

Then there was Natalie.

No matter how much chaos ensued, she never lost her cool. How did she do it? Why did he find her talents so damned aggravating? Not only did she have the patience of a saint, but the more focused she'd become on restoring order to the Buckhorn home, the more attractive to him she'd become. Her messy ponytails and rumpled T-shirts and jeans were offset by a quiet strength he found himself craving.

Warm sun streamed through the western wall of his house, reminding him of the promise he'd made to help Natalie with the twins.

By sheer will, could he make tonight different? The next two weeks before he *would* leave? Instead of resenting Natalie's abilities with his nieces, could he learn to become more like her?

When they'd been kids, Daisy's favorite toy had been her Magic 8 Ball. Wyatt couldn't say what made him flash back on that now, but regardless, he feared the answer to his current question, after a fervent shake, would be *outlook doubtful.*

"OKAY, DADDY! SORRY you talk funny, but I love you, too!"

That afternoon, Bonnie and Betsy hung up their house phone extensions at the same time. They'd spent the past ten minutes talking with their parents, and while Natalie could tell the conversation had done the girls good, Bonnie's current frown had her worried.

"What are you thinking, sweetie?"

From her perch on a kitchen counter stool, Bonnie sighed. "Daddy and Mommy sound sick, but why can't they be sick here?"

"Yeah." Betsy joined her sister. "I say that, too."

"Because they are hurt pretty bad, they have to stay at the hospital where there are lots of doctors and nurses to fix them."

"But Mommy at least sounds normal," Bonnie said. "Why can't she come home?"

Natalie surveyed the freezer for what to cook for dinner. "Remember last year when you two got stomach flu?"

"Yeah…" the twins said in unison.

"You felt awful, but still looked adorable, right?"

"We are very cute," Bonnie noted.

"And we have the longest hair in our class," Betsy said.

"There you have it. You proved my point. Just because you were still pretty didn't mean you felt great. That's how your mom is."

"Oh." Bonnie frowned.

"Guess that makes sense," Betsy said.

Finding a two-pound chub of ground beef, Natalie decided tacos sounded yummy and simple. Plus, she remembered seeing corn tortillas at the back of the fridge.

She put the meat in the microwave to thaw, then assembled lettuce, tomatoes and cheese on the counter.

Mabel sat at the table, squeezing Play-Doh.

Esther lounged on her play mat, "talking" to the pink pigs dangling from an arch.

"Can we help?" Betsy asked.

"Absolutely. But first, wash your hands."

The back door opened and in strolled Wyatt.

If Natalie hadn't known him her whole life, his stubbled square jawline and killer white-toothed smile would've been major turn-ons. Alas, his good looks would never fool her into thinking he might be a good catch.

He hung his cowboy hat on a wall hook, and then turned to the girls. "Wanna play Monopoly?"

Bonnie shook her head. "We're cooking."

Betsy said, "Thanks, Uncle Wyatt, but Miss Natalie's way more fun than you."

Natalie fully expected him to turn right around and leave. Instead, he surprised her by picking up his niece in a growling hug. "If you like Miss Nat better, then that means I'll have to eat you for dinner!"

"No!" Bonnie jumped at his side. "Eat me! Me!"

A growling, laughing chase ensued with all three of them dashing behind her. When Wyatt passed, he brushed against Natalie's backside. Sparks of awareness were impossible to deny.

Even Mabel wanted in on the fun, waving her hands and shouting, "Me! Me!"

Wyatt hefted the toddler onto his shoulders and proceeded to chase the twins into the living room, growling all the way. Soon, sounds of thumping and shrieking came from upstairs.

Natalie couldn't imagine what had gotten into Wyatt for him to do such a behavioral one-eighty, but she had to admit she liked the change.

Out of breath and laughing, they all eventually landed back in the kitchen, joining Mabel at the table to make Play-Doh cakes and cookies.

Kolt and Luke stopped by with Callie, unashamed to admit they were missing Daisy and hoping to snag a free meal.

When everyone had eaten their fill, Natalie moved to clear the table, but Luke and Kolt stopped her.

"You cooked," Luke said. "Least we can do is clean."

"Thank you, both." Natalie ambushed Kolt with a hug. Turning to Mabel and Esther, she said, "With my free time, you two are getting your baths."

"Let me do it." Wyatt took Esther from her carrier.

"Do you know how?" Natalie didn't ask to be snide, she genuinely needed to know before turning over her best friend's children to their clueless bachelor uncle.

Holding squirming Mabel under his arm, he said,

"How tough can it be? Like washing a car, only smaller, right?"

"If you say so."

The second Wyatt was out of earshot, Luke said, "You might want to keep an eye on him. I'm not sure who's in more trouble—the girls or my brother-in-law."

FACED WITH A PLETHORA of bath toys and seats and lotions, Wyatt wasn't sure the pep talk he'd given himself on being a better uncle would be enough to see him through his voluntary task. From the looks of it, bath time may be more complex than he'd anticipated.

Setting Mabel on her feet, he asked, "Can you tell Uncle Wyatt what we're supposed to do?"

She pointed at a pink rubber duck. "Ducky says quack!"

"Thanks," he said, ignoring the ball of fear in his gut. "That helps a lot."

She pointed to a boat. "Boat goes *brrrrrooooom!*"

"Esther, I don't suppose you have any clearer advice?"

The infant blew a raspberry.

Okay—well, water would be a great first start, but he wasn't sure on the temperature. Seemed like one of the women he'd dated had told him her niece screamed whenever her water was even lukewarm. Personally, he enjoyed a near-scalding shower, but that had to hurt baby skin.

Wyatt couldn't help but smile when Mabel had already stripped and climbed into a purple plastic bath chair in the tub.

"Bubbles!" She pointed to a giant bottle of Mr. Bubble.

A knock sounded on the door. Natalie asked, "How's it going?"

He scratched his head. "We're good except for water temp. Thoughts?"

"That is tricky." On her way to the tub, she overwhelmed him with her trademark scent of watermelon lotion, along with lingering traces of her delicious dinner. She squatted to adjust the faucet, revealing a yellow polka-dot thong. "What you'll want to do is run your wrist under the warm water, like this. Checking to ensure it's not too hot. Make sense?"

The only thing that made any sense to Wyatt was Natalie removing her jeans to give him a better look at how little she wore in the way of panties.

Two weeks...

If he could keep his eye on the prize of freedom to be gained in those fourteen days, he'd no longer need worry about the naughty thoughts that had a way of popping into his head whenever she was around. As a woman growing more pregnant by the day, she was the enemy. Last thing he needed was her nonverbal reminder of the one thing he wanted, but would never have.

Mouth dry, he nodded. "Got it."

While the tub filled and Mabel splashed, Natalie said, "Esther's the tricky one. As you can see, Mabel knows the drill.

"Set Esther's seat in the tub, preferably on the opposite end as her sister. Then, you'll want to place her in it. Use a plastic cup to get her wet, then go over her body with the baby wash and rinse. For her hair, there's baby shampoo. Once you finish, she has a special towel—" she pointed to a hooded pink hippo hanging on the wall "—just put it over her head and pat her nice and dry. Then you add lotion, a fresh diaper, pajamas and *voilà,* you have a baby ready for bed."

"How'd you learn to do all of this?"

Her helpful smile faded. "You know Josie had a daughter with her first husband, right?"

Wyatt nodded. "Dallas mentioned it."

"Emma was Josie's life. Josie's been my best friend since the day she came to town, and she shared every precious moment of raising her baby with me. It was fun. But losing Emma was—" Natalie looked away, swiping tears. "Sorry. Raging hormones have me crying at everything from Hallmark commercials to roadkill."

"It's okay."

"Bubbles!" Mabel demanded from the tub.

"Guess we should get back to work," Natalie said, taking Esther from him, removing her tiny clothes.

"Let me do that," Wyatt said, easing alongside Natalie in the tight space. "Since we're in this together for a couple more weeks, I need to learn."

She cast him a questioning look, but thankfully didn't speak. Instead, she lined up all of the potions he'd need, handed him a fresh washcloth and then did something he couldn't begin to understand: without a word, she cupped his shoulder, kissed the top of his head and then left the room.

Chapter Eight

When Natalie left the cramped space she'd shared with Wyatt and the kids, she was trembling. In the moment her gaze had locked with Wyatt's, he'd told her without saying a word that he truly, deeply cared about the children in their charge. He'd told her that for all of his bluster, he did have a heart—more than he wanted anyone to know. Especially her.

In the kitchen, she made a cup of mint tea.

She wiped the counters free of the crumbs Luke and Kolt had missed.

Most of all, she waited. From upstairs came muffled sounds of laughter that made her wonder all the more at Wyatt's sudden transformation. Why had he chosen tonight to fully engage in not only Esther's care, but his other three nieces', as well?

When Wyatt finally ambled down the back staircase, Natalie pounced. "What's wrong with you?"

"Excuse me?"

With Luke and the big kids in the movie room with explosions blaring, she felt safe to say exactly what was on her mind. "You're a walking contradiction. One minute, your actions—your whole demeanor—are in attack mode. The next, you're this warm, loving uncle trying to do his best by these little girls. Which man are you? Because at the moment, I'm confused."

"Look," he said on his way to the fridge. "I'll be first to admit I'm far from perfect, but then who is? All I can do is try to make up for past mistakes and, Nat, a lot of those include the way I've acted around you."

Not sure what to say, she bowed her head.

"After Esther's christening, you and I shared a connection—based on mutual frustration with our families, but still there." He removed a beer only to set it on the counter. Now he stood behind her. Not touching her, but close enough for heat and awareness to shimmer as if their bodies were hot blacktop on an endless summer day. "I'm tired, Nat. I need—" He sharply exhaled. "Ever since I found out I could never father a child, I've worked hard to distance myself from damn near everyone I encounter. Not sure how or even why, but it dawned on me that the effort is exhausting. I'm tired of fighting. I just want to live, you know. Stop worrying about it."

Though the counselor in Natalie longed to turn around and give Wyatt a hug, the woman Craig's sweet words had destroyed was wary. How many times had Craig told her what she wanted to hear, only to get what he wanted, then, when it served him, walk away? She wasn't sure what Wyatt could possibly want from her—surely not casual sex—but what? Could it be as simple as him needing a genuine friend?

If so, in her turbulent hormonal state, was there anything simple about the way she'd been feeling whenever the man was near?

While giving the girls their bath, she'd caught a glimpse of him she'd only dreamt about. She'd never denied his being handsome. Or the way her body hummed with awareness whenever he was around. Part of her wanted him to be aware of her, too. But not in superficial ways such as thinking she had great hair and eyes, but on a deeper level. She wanted him to appreciate the accomplished woman she'd become. But why? Because no matter how many signals her body sent to steal another kiss, her conscience knew he was wrong for her in every conceivable way.

"You're too quiet." Wyatt finally uncapped his beer to take a swig. Back to the fridge, he removed the leftover taco meat, took a spoon from the nearest drawer and proceeded to feast. "Makes me suspicious. Like you're plotting my demise."

Covering her face with her hands, she shook her head. "You make me crazy."

"Trust me, the feeling's mutual." Setting his snack to the counter, he crossed to her, taking her hands in his. "Kissing you at Esther's christening was a mistake. *Huge.*"

Heart racing, Natalie wanted to admit to feeling the same, but her brain was so focused on his nearness—the scent of tacos and beer on his warm breath—that her mouth no longer worked.

"Because ever since then, regardless of how many times a day we bicker, all I want to do is this..." Lowering his lips to hers, what this kiss lacked in showiness, it made up for in layer upon layer of emotion. The sweetness could've made her weep. The unmasked wanting made her incapable of denying how badly she wanted more. To know him skin to skin.

Dizzying, thrilling moments later, he drew back. The intensity in his eyes read as a challenge. As if he dared her to deny what they'd shared hadn't been amazing.

She looked down only to realize she'd fisted his shirt and now clung to him for support. Her legs had long since gone rubbery and her lungs no longer seemed to work.

He kissed her again, and their bold sweep of tongues did nothing to help her return to reality long enough to push him away. "Damn, you taste good. Like candy I've been teased with for decades and only just now got to taste."

"But this doesn't change anything," she reminded. "You and me are pals—nothing more."

"Woman," he brushed his lips against the base of her throat, in the process sending shimmering pleasure coursing through her body, "you talk too damned much."

Agreed. But someone needed to be the voice of logic before they both ended up doing something they'd regret in the morning. Though, a long-buried part of her wondered if she woke in Wyatt's arms would she crave doing it again and again?

"Eeeeeew!" Bonnie and Betsy cried in unison.

Bonnie took her protest a step further by asking, "Uncle Wyatt, why are your hands on Miss Natalie's butt?"

LONG AFTER LUKE AND KOLT left, after the twins had finally drifted off to sleep, Wyatt tossed and turned in the guest room. He was too hot, and pushed back the covers. Then he was cold. His pillows were too flat. He grabbed extra from the bed's empty side, but then they were too tall.

Growling in frustration, he sat up and scratched his chest.

Usually, he went right to sleep, so what was the problem?

A sassy brunette flashed before his mind's eye. She wore her pregnancy beautifully. Some future moms were sick the whole time and complexions blotchy, but not Natalie. Her skin glowed. Her eyes were bright. Over the years, he'd been with many incredibly beautiful women. Natalie didn't have conventional looks. She had an inner glow he found far more intriguing than the usual great rack.

But why? Not only was he on the verge of leaving the country, but she represented the one thing he was trying to escape. In acknowledging her magnetic pull, he'd become a walking contradiction. He said he wanted nothing more than to never see another pregnant woman, but in Natalie's case, he couldn't get enough.

Pushing to his feet, he adjusted the fly of his boxers, then opened his bedroom door, creeping down the hall to her room.

Once there, he should've knocked, but didn't.

Feet soundless on thick carpet, he crawled in bed alongside her, bunching pillows beneath his head before giving her shoulder a gentle nudge. "Natalie? You awake?"

Dressed in an old-fashioned flannel nightgown, she bolted upright, hugging the sheet to her chest. "What are you doing, scaring me half to death? In case you haven't noticed, I'm about a hundred months pregnant. At the worst I could have the baby right now, or at best, pee the bed."

He laughed. "Sorry. Need me to change the sheets?"

"No," she said with an outraged smack to his bare chest.

Under different circumstances, he would've trapped

her hand with his, but Wyatt figured he was already in enough hot water.

"Get out. Seriously."

"I will," he promised, easing up onto his elbow. "Just give me a minute."

"For what?"

"Truth? Your kiss has me all hot and bothered and—"

"*My* kiss?" She coughed. "I was ambushed."

"Sugar," he flashed his best cocky cowboy smile, "it's a little late to plead innocence. You were just as into it."

"Maybe I was, but that doesn't give you the right to barge into my bed, expecting more."

"Bit presumptuous, Miss Lewis. I'm solely here to talk."

She pummeled him again.

Grabbing her wrists, he pulled her in for a replay of their dessert. Only this time, with fewer clothes between them, her breasts mounded soft and full against his chest, causing an erection that was both pleasure and pain.

"No," she moaned, pushing him away only to pull him back.

"I agree." Yet he couldn't stop kissing her.

After a deep sigh, she pulled back. "Talk. Th-that's why you're here, right?"

"Yeah." Heels of his hands to his forehead, he said, "Okay, so we've been fixtures in each other's lives for so long we're like furniture, right?"

"Way to make me feel special."

"You know what I mean. I've always considered you a good-looking woman, but since kissing you at Esther's christening, I can't stop thinking of you in terms of someone I want to know better—only, that's no good. You're Natalie. You deserve to be treated like someone special. Only I'm in no position to give anything other than meaningless sex." He wished for more lighting so he could see her expression.

"This the part where I confess that's all I want, too? Just a quick tickle and poke?" After a sharp laugh, she said, "We have chemistry. Big deal. It doesn't mean anything. We don't mean anything."

She was right. So how come deep inside he feared ignoring his growing fascination with her would be wrong?

"HE DIDN'T," CAMI SAID over lunch in Natalie's office later that week. While Esther slept in her carrier, Mabel rummaged through the toy chest Natalie kept on hand for times when visiting parents brought younger siblings. Though Natalie was on an indefinite leave of absence, she'd been cooped up at the ranch for so long with Wyatt that she'd desperately needed out. "What did you say?"

Natalie covered her flushed face with her hands. "I don't remember. I was so mortified by his even being there, let alone kissing me, I couldn't think straight. A few minutes later, he left, and I spent the rest of the night staring at the ceiling."

Cami took a bite of her chicken salad. "Wonder what Josie would say about this development?"

"I'd love to know, but the last thing I want her worrying about is an event this irrelevant."

"How is the best kiss you've ever had irrelevant?"

"Because," Natalie said, stabbing her fork through a cherry tomato, "regardless of how much I enjoyed what happened between Wyatt and me, it will never happen again."

"What if it does?" Cami's eyebrows raised in challenge. "Are you strong enough to resist full-force Buckhorn charm?"

The question made Natalie's pulse race, but did nothing to diminish her resolve. "Here's the thing—Wyatt's leaving. I'm having Craig's baby alone because I stupidly believed our child would be the glue needed to bind us together. With Wyatt, even if I wanted something more than those few kisses, I'm smart enough to know there's not even a question of whether or not he may one day leave. His flight's already scheduled. Trust me, from now until the day he goes, this little flirtation we've been playing with is done."

"Luke tells me you and Nat have been hooking up." Cash hefted a hay bale from the truck bed to the south pasture feeding area. Though the temperature was chilly, the sun packed enough heat to bring out a sweat.

"Where'd you hear that?" Wyatt slung his next bale with extra force. He was already tired from no sleep. Last thing he needed was for his business to be spread all over hell and creation.

"Bonnie told Kolt she found you two doing *it*. Kolt told his dad. His dad told me."

"This family does love to gossip." Removing his hat, Wyatt wiped his forehead with the sleeve of his denim shirt. "First, all we were doing is making out. And second, Bonnie needs her mouth washed out with soap."

"No need to get defensive. I'm just making conversation."

In the midst of snorting, mooing and chewing cattle,

they unloaded the last remaining bales in silence, then used knives to slit the bailing twine, gathering it all before climbing back into the truck.

"You do know," Cash said, removing his leather work gloves and slapping them to the dash, "since Nat's practically family, you can't use her for sex. Plus, she's pregnant. I get the turn-on factor—Wren was seriously hot with my baby in her oven. But Nat's baby isn't even yours, which makes you dipping in that particular pond like poaching."

To keep from punching his little brother, Wyatt gripped the wheel especially hard. The old road had enough dips and deep tire ruts to warrant his full attention. "Not that what I do is any of your business, but for the last time, there's nothing going on between me and Nat."

Cash snorted. "Then why were your hands all over Nat's ass?"

"Bonnie needs a good old-fashioned spanking."

"No doubt about it, but my question still stands."

"All right, look, we've shared a few hot times, but that's it. Call it an experiment gone bad. We've both made it plain it goes no further. End of story."

"If you say so." Cash's sarcastic tone made it clear he wasn't buying the line Wyatt was selling. "Just keep in mind Nat happens to be Josie's best friend. You piss off Nat, you piss off your sister-in-law, which pisses off Dallas. Last thing you need is him breathing fire down your neck."

"Stop," Wyatt said with a narrowed-eyed, sideways glare. "I'm a grown man and will make out with whomever I please, whenever I please. Dallas can huff and puff all he wants, but I seriously don't give a—"

"Watch out!"

Wyatt swerved to avoid hitting a winter calf, in the process ramming the right front tire onto a jagged stump. Freakin' swell. Now, he not only had a busted tire to deal with, but more time with his little brother.

"If you're as bad with women," Cash noted, "as you are at driving, no wonder you can't make lasting magic happen with Nat. Now, if you happened to be as good-looking as me, then—"

"Unless you want that pretty face of yours marred with a black eye, you really ought to shut up."

"LET ME FEED MABEL," Natalie was surprised to hear Wyatt say two nights later. "You handle the twins and yourself."

Esther had already been fed her bottle and cooed at the mobile dangling over her carrier.

"I'm not a baby." Bonnie shoveled mashed potatoes into her mouth. "I feed myself."

Not to be outdone, Betsy said, "Me, too."

"I know you two will be fine," their uncle encouraged Mabel to use a spoon for her peas, "but you know how messy Miss Nat can be when she doesn't concentrate."

"Uh-huh." Bonnie nodded.

"Gee, thanks." Natalie helped herself to seconds of meat loaf, hoping nice, warm comfort food counteracted the cool look she cast Wyatt's way. To the twins, she said, "You two talked to your mom a long time. What did she say?"

Betsy bounced on her seat. "Daddy and her are excited to see us and Mommy wants to know if we have our Christmas tree up yet, because it's only two weeks until Santa comes and everyone knows he gets grumpy if you don't have a tree."

"Yeah, and Kolt's been *real* bad," Bonnie said, "so we'll have to have an extra big and fancy tree."

"Shouldn't you spend more time worrying about your own behavior and less about your cousin's?" Wyatt had cut Mabel's meat into bite-size chunks. She pitched two at Kitty, who gobbled them up.

"Santa knows I'm perfect," Bonnie said.

"Me, too." Betsy tossed at least a dozen peas to the cat.

Accidentally catching the sparkle in Wyatt's eyes caused Natalie's pulse to quicken. Her body refused to get the memo that she wanted nothing to do with him. Still, it was fun to share a *parental* moment.

Wyatt asked, "Wouldn't Santa want Kolt's tree to be at Kolt's house?"

The twins leaned together for a whispered conference, at the end of which Bonnie announced, "We think because Kolt's bad and we're good, we'll help make Santa extra happy. If he has two trees, then that'd be even better."

"Yeah," Betsy said, "and we think if we have three or four trees here at our house, then that would even help the bad babies get a good Christmas."

"I don't know about having that many," Wyatt said, "but if it's all right with Miss Nat, how about when you two get home from school tomorrow, we head out to the tree patch for at least one?"

"Yay!" Both girls abandoned their meals to dance.

After dishes were done and the babies were bathed and sweetly sleeping, after the twins were supposedly asleep, but actually playing Barbies with flashlights under their covers, Natalie curled onto a corner of the sofa with Josie's well-loved copy of *What to Expect When You're Expecting.*

She'd just gotten engrossed on the horrors of gestational diabetes when she looked up to find Wyatt staring.

"Chilly in here," he said. "Want me to make a fire?"

"That'd be nice. Thanks."

While he worked, she tried settling back into her reading, but the view of his broad shoulders and strong back was too darned distracting.

Worse yet, once he'd finished, he sat on the opposite end of her sofa with what looked like an exhilarating geography tome.

Natalie had read on to preeclampsia when Wyatt asked, "Need popcorn?"

"No, thank you."

"A drink?" he suggested. "Wine? Mom's got the good stuff. She won't notice if we share a bottle."

"What are we? In junior high? And anyway, in case you forgot, I'm pregnant."

He slapped his book to the sofa. "I'm trying here, okay?"

"To do what?" She rested her read on the sofa arm.

"For us to have a nice, normal night. In a little over a week, I'll be gone, but until then, I want to experience what it's like being a family."

She frowned. "Why?"

"Because for the first time in forever, I'm excited about getting a Christmas tree. I can't wait for all of us to trek into the woods. I know it sounds stupid, but—"

"No…" Turning to face him, she bowed her head. "I feel the same. But it's pointless. You're leaving. I'm staying. Our roles will never change. We're wired differently. Maybe that's what's driving the attraction, but—"

"You're feeling it, too?"

"To a maddening degree," she admitted. "But I'm on the verge of becoming a mother. If I can't resist temptation, how am I supposed to teach that skill to my child?"

"I see your point."

"Good." Gravitating closer, she managed, "We're both rational adults. As such, I think we can manage to give the girls a special holiday without giving in to base urges."

"Agreed." So why were they slowly coming together until nothing but mutually hitched breaths stood between them? Why did their lips press together? Exquisitely soft and tender and sweet enough to feel the intensity clear to her toes. When sensation took over, all reason vanished. Sanity was replaced with the sweep of Wyatt's tongue, stroking her into a sort of fevered madness she felt helpless to deny.

Once necessity caused her to pause for breath, Natalie put her hands on Wyatt's chest, hoping she'd summon the strength to push him away. "No."

"Sorry," he said, also breathing heavy.

"Me, too."

"So from here on out, we won't do this anymore."

"Definitely not." She crushed him in a hug, resisting the urge to nip his earlobe. "We should do our best to get along in a strictly platonic manner."

Skimming his hand under her flannel sweatshirt, her satin-smooth baby bump put him in a state of male distress.

"Mmm…" she moaned, "that feels nice."

"No kidding."

Her lips again landed on his, rendering him incapable of doing anything but easing his free hand to her neck to press her closer.

Suddenly, there was an alien-like movement beneath his palm. Drawing back, he asked, "Was that—him—or her? Inside you?"

Eyes wide, as if searching his expression to discover if he'd been put off or moved by the notion of making out with a woman pregnant with another man's baby, she nodded. "I think *he* likes you."

"He?" Wyatt barely managed to whisper past his tight throat. "You're having a son?"

She nodded. "I found out at my latest ultrasound. I thought I wanted to be surprised, but at the last minute changed my mind. You're the first person I've told."

In Wyatt's every fantasy about having a family, he'd always wanted a son. Which only made his current situation harder. "Thank you—for trusting me. I'm happy for you."

Tears shone in her eyes. "Me, too. I mean, I'm happy. But then sometimes I'm really scared. Like what am I doing? Believing I'm smart enough to raise a child."

Acting on instinct, he took her hand in his, giving her a squeeze. "Judging by the way you've cared for Dallas and Josie's crew, you're going to be fine. Perfect."

"Think so?" Her voice had gone small. Like she truly didn't know how impressive her mothering skills were.

"The first night we were charged with caring for the entire Buckhorn brood, and all the babies were screaming, I freaked out. You, however, acted as if you'd never met an infant you didn't love. And they love you back. Your baby boy is going to believe the sun rises and sets in your arms."

Her body fell limp against him. "You don't know what a relief it is to hear from someone—anyone—that they think I can do this. My parents are freaking out about me not being married. Before the accident, even Josie told me I could move in here if I couldn't manage raising a baby on my own."

He couldn't help but laugh. "Sure your parents haven't conferred with my mom? Sounds like the same line she fed both my brothers and sister. I swear the woman won't be happy until she's married off the entire county."

"Why does everyone think wedding rings are the only path to happiness? I've been fine on my own for years. Why wouldn't I be just as fine with a child?"

"You will be."

Natalie's hug evoked an emotion deep inside him. Wyatt felt important and needed and as if his mere act of supporting her when no one else had made a genuine difference.

"Thank you," she sniffled through tears.

"I didn't do anything."

"Yes, Wyatt, you did. I've been sitting here, reading this stupid book about everything that can go wrong with my pregnancy. You reminded me how right finally holding my son will be."

Wyatt thought, *Wish I'd be around to meet him.*

Chapter Nine

"I don't like this one," Bonnie whined with a stomp of her red rain boots.

Betsy stomped her pink boots. "I do!"

"Ladies..." Natalie warned. "Santa's watching."

After a thirty-minute truck ride down a bone-rattling dirt trail, then tromping through a field cloaked by freezing drizzle, they'd finally reached the Christmas tree plot that'd been planted by the first Buckhorns in Oklahoma. Each generation was responsible for reseeding, and now a pine forest stood, wind whispering through the fragrant boughs.

Bonnie said, "Santa doesn't like ugly trees!"

"You're the ugly one," Betsy said. "And I hate your red boots!"

"I hate your pink ones!"

Fingers to his mouth, Wyatt blew an earsplitting whistle.

Mabel, who rode high on his shoulders, squealed, holding her hands to her ears.

Esther, who'd been asleep in her papoose-style carrier, snug against Natalie's chest, woke with a start, screaming loud enough to prompt a flock of crows into cawing flight.

"Shhh," Natalie soothed. "You're okay. Only the big girls are in trouble."

"Santa hates you," Bonnie informed her sister.

Betsy stuck out her tongue.

"Knock it off," Wyatt said. "If I were Santa, I'd bring you two a bowl of rocks."

"It's s'posed to be a bag of switches," Betsy said. "You have to get Santa's stuff right, Uncle Wyatt."

He glanced Natalie's way to catch her grinning. "Yeah, Uncle Wyatt. Get it right."

It'd been two days since the intimacies they'd shared in Georgina's living room. Two days during which nothing, and yet everything had changed. Wyatt was no longer her enemy, but her friend. And it was nice. Yet fragile and disconcerting. Somewhat like a dream she wasn't entirely sure she wanted to wake from.

"Oh," he said, "it'll be right when we go home with no tree and you two spend the rest of the night in your room."

Both girls pouted with their arms folded tight across their chests.

"Miss Nat," Wyatt asked, Mabel once again all smiles on his shoulders, "how about you and this little lady pick the tree?"

Gazing across a sea of green pines and firs, low clouds hugging the hills, Natalie pointed to her favorite, asking the toddler, "Mabel, sweetie, do you like that one?"

"Ice cream!"

"Ow! Hey, kid, take it easy on your poor uncle." Wyatt rubbed the sides of his head where she'd slapped her excitement.

"Pumpkin," Natalie reached for the girl's hands, trying to calm her, "I'm not sure where you see ice cream, but I'm taking your enthusiasm to mean we've chosen our official Christmas tree."

"Yay!" the fickle twins cried. "It's pretty!"

Wyatt set Mabel on her feet next to Natalie, then commenced with cutting. In a way, it was sad seeing the tree coming down, but watching him work his ax proved insanely hot. Granted, Weed Gulch had its fair share of manly men, but whew, Wyatt had them all beat. With each strike, he had a habit of sticking his tongue—just the tip—to his upper lip. Alas, the show didn't last long, as all too soon he'd finished his task and was dragging their prize to the truck.

"Ride," Mabel said, running alongside him, pointing to his shoulders.

He scooped her back to her former position, keeping a careful hold. His contagious chuckle and slow grin stole Natalie's breath.

Esther snug and still sleeping against her, the twins giggling and running around their uncle, Natalie found it all too easy to picture a scene not so different from this in her own future. For all her resolve to steer clear of men, she'd be lying if she didn't admit to having the occasional craving for domestic bliss. Fortunately, she was smart enough to realize times like these were a rarity and not the norm.

At the house, while the twins and Mabel ran wild, singing "Jingle Bells," she and Wyatt tackled taking ornament and decoration boxes from the attic. Esther helped by lying sweetly in her portable playpen, blowing raspberries at dust bunnies. Considering Georgina typically had a team of Tulsa florists and decorators prepare the house for the holidays, the only items Natalie was concerned with were family keepsakes.

"I've always loved the Buckhorn way of celebrating

the holidays," Natalie said to Wyatt, fingering raised lettering on a Baby's First Christmas ball.

Grunting while passing Natalie a dusty box, Wyatt said, "When I was a kid, holidays were insane. Seemed like my folks went to a different party every night in December." Sitting on an old chest, he rubbed his whisker-stubbled jaw. "The one they hosted here every year was nothing like the kid-friendly fests we have now. Back in the day, we're talking black tie and limos stretched down the entire drive. The year Reagan came I'm surprised the Secret Service didn't take out Dallas and Luke when they used BB guns to appoint themselves official backup."

Natalie said, "As an outsider looking in, the Buckhorns seemed like royalty."

"Nah. We had our issues. Hell—still do."

"Yeah, but what's it like to never worry about normal things? Say during the holidays when I want to buy my mom an extra special gift, but the gas bill is so high, I don't have the cash."

Resting his elbows on his knees, he cradled his forehead on the heels of his palms. "That old saying about money not buying happiness? It's true. When Mom lost Dad, I thought we'd lose her, too."

"Everybody struggles with losing loved ones. I'm talking about day-to-day drudgery. Like do you ever crave steak for dinner, but end up with mac and cheese?"

"I love that stuff." Easing upright, he rubbed the back of his neck. "When I was ten, we went skiing in the Alps and the chef in the castle Dad rented made it with Gruyère and lobster."

"Seriously?"

He laughed. "Yeah, but all I'm saying is the Buckhorns are far from perfect. My dad was a great man, but looking back on it, I didn't really know him. If I told you some of the stuff keeps me up nights, you'd be glad for money woes."

"I'll bite."

"I had it first!" Bonnie shouted.

Betsy said, "Your Barbie doesn't even like that dress!"

"I want cookie!" At the base of the attic stairs, Natalie caught a glimpse of the twins playing tug-of-war with a scrap of hot pink fabric.

Mabel hopped back and forth between them.

Esther seemed happy enough, cooing at a stuffed cow.

"Hold that thought," Natalie said. "Looks like my services are needed as a referee."

"THERE YOU GO, SWEETIE." That night, Wyatt held Mabel as high as his arms reached. In her grubby hands was the battered gold star that had topped the Buckhorn family Christmas tree for as long as he could remember. "Put it right on top."

"Star, star, star!" For a little squirt, she did a great job. Her grin warmed him through and through. Spending so much time with his nieces had helped Wyatt see the girls in a new light. Sure, they were infinitely more trouble than he'd thought, but times like these, when even the twins were pitching in and doing a good job, he experienced a gut-level connection to all of them he'd never expected.

If he felt this attached to them when they weren't even his, he couldn't imagine how it must feel for Dallas, Cash or Luke having children born of their own DNA.

"Uncle Wyatt, look at this one." Betsy held up a salt-dough candy cane. Josie had helped the girls make them in their kindergarten class.

"Mine's better," Bonnie said, holding hers up, as well.

"They're both gorgeous," Natalie said. Taking the tissue from what Wyatt knew was Josie's favorite angel, she put it on a high branch. Dallas had told him Josie purchased the ornament the first holiday after her little girl had died. "I'm sure your mom and dad are sorry they're missing out on this."

"Yeah." Bonnie sat on the hearth in front of the crackling fire. "I sure miss them. When are they coming home?"

Natalie wrapped the girl in a hug. "Just as soon as they start feeling better."

"Wanna watch a movie?" Betsy asked her sister. "This isn't as much fun without Daddy and Mommy."

Bonnie nodded.

Mabel's interest had turned to playing with foil garland and Esther had fallen asleep.

While Wyatt and Natalie finished the tree in companionable silence, Bing Crosby crooned carols. Though it was only a little past six, darkness had already fallen. On his own with Natalie, Wyatt wasn't sure what to say. In the attic, if the twins hadn't interrupted, he'd found himself wanting to share his misgivings about leaving. He'd been around her so much, sharing everything with her felt not only natural, but normal. Putting ornaments on the tree had always been a special event, reserved for family only. But in ways, he felt almost closer to her than he did them. Not good for a man sworn to forever remain a bachelor.

"I don't mean to pry," Natalie said, "but earlier,

when you told me you have worries, is there anything I can do to help?"

"How did I know you wouldn't let that go?"

"Had I said the same, would you?"

Laughing, he admitted, "Probably not."

"Well?" she probed.

He added three more ornaments before saying, "I shouldn't have brought it up."

"Now that you did, don't leave me hanging."

"I leave in a few days." He added another ornament to the tree. "I was psyched about my trip. Dallas and Josie are on the mend. No reason for me to put off leaving any longer, right? Except for you. I feel like I'd be shirking my responsibility—leaving you with all these kids and the monstrosity of a house."

"You asking for my blessing to go?"

He hung two purple reindeer. "Guess I am. If you feel it's too much for you, what with the baby, I'll call the whole thing off."

"And leave me with the guilt of knowing I stopped you from going on the trip of a lifetime?" A sharp laugh escaped her. "No, thanks."

They finished the tree in silence, rain drumming the skylights.

Once the twins were tucked in bed, Wyatt wanted to ask Natalie to join him by the fire. They could talk or play cards. Anything. Didn't matter. He wanted to spend time with her. But the general vibe wasn't conducive to a night of casually hanging out. In offering to stay, he thought he'd be doing her a favor. Instead, he got the impression his offer had royally pissed her off. Had she thought he didn't have confidence in her to handle their impromptu family on her own? If so, nothing could be further from the truth. In fact, he feared the true heart of the matter was that he dreaded leaving—not just her, but his nieces. The newfound feeling of being needed was intoxicating.

In the hall outside the twins' closed bedroom Natalie yawned, politely covering her mouth. "I don't know about you, but I'm ready to call it a night."

"It's only nine."

"In case you haven't noticed, I'm carrying a linebacker inside me. I'm exhausted."

Wyatt wanted to touch her belly again. Feel her son move. "Anything I can do for you? Make tea? Rub your feet?"

"No, thanks."

"You're not upset with me, are you?"

"Over what?" She paused in front of her bedroom door.

"Offering to stay. Give me the word, and I will—but not because I don't think you can handle everything just fine on your own."

"You're sweet, but no. Our trip to the hospital tomorrow will be rough. We should be well-rested for not only the girls, but Josie and Dallas. Last thing I want them worrying about is if we're up for the task of caring for their children—even though you are only a short-timer."

"Right." Was he a fool for feeling rejected? As if they were back in high school and he'd asked Natalie to a big dance, only to have her turn him down? Shoving his hands in his jean pockets, he said, "Guess I'll use this quiet time to go through some mail."

"Okay…well." She flopped her hands at her sides. "See you in the morning."

There was so much he wanted to say. He wanted reassurance she truly was tired and not avoiding him.

Most of all, he wanted to hold her. Or maybe for her to hold him.

Instead, he flashed an awkward wave.

She retreated to her room.

He spent the next four hours pouting over beer and football.

NATALIE HAD THOUGHT SHE WAS prepared for seeing Josie and Dallas. She was wrong. Though their facial bruises were fading, they still looked deathly pale and were hooked up to a myriad of equipment she didn't begin to understand. Due to light sensitivity, the shades had been drawn. The room reeked of antiseptic.

For the moment, Mabel and Esther had stayed in the waiting room with their grandmother.

The twins had tight hold of Natalie's hands.

Bonnie whispered, "Mommy, what's wrong with you and why won't Daddy wake up?"

Betsy said, "Yeah. I wanna know, too."

Wyatt clung to a dark corner, arms crossed, expression grim.

Josie winced through a small smile. "Daddy's tired, but his doctors say that before you know it, he's going to be fine—me, too. All we want you two to worry about is your schoolwork. And your holiday concert."

"Wish you could be there." Betsy bravely stepped forward, reaching for Josie's hand, but there was an IV. The little girl settled for holding her stepmom's fingers.

"Me, too, sweetheart. But Miss Natalie and Uncle Wyatt will be there, and they'll tape the whole show so your dad and I don't miss a thing."

"Uncle Wyatt can't go. He's leaving."

"Oh?" Josie looked to Natalie, who flashed her an exaggerated bright, confident smile. Monday morning,

Wyatt would head out—this time with nothing holding him back. Especially not unwarranted worries about her.

Bonnie said, "This place is scary. Why can't you come home?"

"We will," Josie promised. "Real soon."

Her friend's posture and weak voice told Natalie no matter how badly Josie might crave being around her girls, she wasn't well enough to handle them all at once.

Josie asked, "C-could you please bring in Mabel? And Esther?"

"Come on, squirts." Wyatt stepped forward to take the twins by their hands. "Let's see what good stuff Grandma has in her purse."

"Love you," Bonnie said to Josie. "Please get better."

"Yeah," Betsy said.

"I will." Josie blew them a kiss.

Sadly, Dallas didn't wake for his daughters' visit and Josie's energy wilted like a cut flower left too long in the sun.

Wyatt and Natalie and the girls took Georgina and Daisy to lunch. The two women appeared exhausted. Not wishing to discuss any topics too heavy in front of the children, they strove for a cheerful holiday vibe, but the twins were smart. They may have wondered about their parents before, but they now knew whatever was going on was serious.

The ride home seemed never-ending, and once there, the twins retreated to their room. Natalie wasn't a big fan of parking small kids in front of a TV, but as she was emotionally spent, she cuddled on her bed with Mabel and Esther. The Disney Channel provided entertainment.

"This a private party?" Wyatt asked, peering in from the hall.

Natalie patted the empty space next to her. "The more the merrier."

After tugging off his cowboy boots and socks, he joined them. "Been a helluva day, hasn't it?"

She nodded. "Not sure what I expected, but what we saw seems worse."

"I know what you mean." He bunched a pillow beneath his head. "I'm used to Dallas being a barking, bossy pain in my you-know-what. When he couldn't wake even to—" Voice cracking, he pressed the heels of his hands to his eyes.

Natalie cradled him to her chest, kissing the top of his head, smoothing his hair. For Wyatt to show this level of vulnerability was beyond uncharacteristic into the realm of heartbreaking.

"Uncle Wyatt, cookie?" Mabel asked.

"No, honey," Natalie said to the girl, stroking, stroking Wyatt's hair. "He doesn't need cookies, just lots of hugs."

Mabel lunged at Wyatt. Even though her chubby arms didn't reach all the way around, her intent was clear. And Natalie, too, succumbed to the emotion of the day. As close as she'd grown to these children—and this man—how was she supposed to first say goodbye to him, then walk away from these beautiful girls when Dallas and Josie did return home? Make no mistake, no one would be more thrilled than Natalie for her dear friend to resume her former life, but how would Natalie deal with the transition from having a family to none? When it was just her and her son, would that family feeling be the same?

"Can I ask you a favor?"

"Sure," Wyatt said. Mabel still clung to his neck.

"I know you have an early flight Monday, but please don't leave without saying goodbye."

Chapter Ten

Four o'clock Monday morning, Wyatt had just emerged from the shower to run a towel over his chest when Esther cried.

He tossed the towel around his neck, stepped into a pair of boxers, then jogged down the hall to take her from her crib. Natalie usually tackled her late-night feedings, but that was around two. He checked her diaper. Loaded.

"Just had to leave me a present before I left, huh?"

In the glow of her Winnie-the-Pooh night-light, Esther cooed on the changing table.

"Wanna know a secret?" he whispered past the knot in his throat. Now an expert with diapers, he unsnapped her onesie and just as efficiently disposed of her dirty diaper and cleaned her mess. "I like to pretend I don't like you—would never want a baby like you for my own—but I'd be lying."

With her lotioned and powdered, he tugged her pj's back down, snapping them snug.

Cradling her, he headed into the adjoining bathroom to wash his hands, then sat in the nursery rocker. "I'm leaving, you know? Before your mom and dad's accident, I thought I knew what I wanted—to run as far from here as I could possibly get. Now, I'm not so sure. I mean, I think I am, but then I see Nat holding you, or playing with Mabel or the twins and I freak. She's beautiful. Not like a model, or that tall Russian I dated last Christmas, but different. This is going to sound crazy, but sometimes I get the feeling her serenity is contagious. It makes me want to emulate her—which is really nutso, because I'm not a nurturing, serene kind of guy."

He took a sideways peek at Esther to find she'd fallen asleep with her thumb in her mouth.

"This a sign I've lost my touch with the ladies?" he teased.

After gently returning her to her crib, for the longest time he stared at the way moonlight kissed her chubby cheeks. Since helping care for Dallas and Josie's crew, he'd stopped dwelling on what he could never have to instead realize what he did. Being a fantastic uncle wouldn't kill him. Instead, he'd have the best of both the family and bachelor worlds. Only, the more he was around Natalie, the more he wondered if maybe his old dating days were no longer for him, either.

The clock was ticking.

He needed to finish packing. Make sure he had his passport and entry visa and a dozen other international travel necessities. He needed to shave and dress and confirm his flight. He needed to do all of that and more, but what did he do? Sit back down in the nursery rocker and watch moonlight fade to sun.

"Wyatt?" Dressed in her nightgown, thick socks and a cap of wild hair, Natalie didn't trust her eyes. "You should be in Dallas by now."

"Yep."

"So why aren't you?" Almost afraid of his answer, she turned her back on him, instead focusing on Esther.

"Couldn't do it. Didn't feel right."

"But *why?*" Facing him, she prayed he couldn't see the relief in her eyes. The moment she'd placed her feet on the floor from the bed, she'd fought a lead weight pressing on her chest. Dread. Regret—for things she had said and hadn't. On some levels, they barely knew each other. On others, she'd always known him. He was as much a part of her as Weed Gulch itself. "I—I hope not because you think I can't cope, because I can. I just—"

Before she could finish her thought, he was on his feet, kissing her. And she let him. Oh, she let him. They kissed and kissed until Esther whimpered and grunted and— "Look!"

Right under their noses, Esther had turned herself over. Judging by her smile, was quite proud of her accomplishment.

"Holy crap," Wyatt said, tickling her tummy. "We have a prodigy on our hands."

Just like that, the questions she had for him were put to the back burner in favor of Esther's amazing skills. If it was this exciting watching her best friend's baby reach a milestone, how fun would it be oohing and aahing over her own?

How sad was it Wyatt would never have that chance?

THURSDAY NIGHT AT THE twins' school Christmas program, Wyatt asked Natalie, "Was it wrong for me to have strong-armed a granny to get these seats?"

"I'd have done the same." With Esther in her carrier, Natalie aimed her camera at the stage. The auditorium had been decorated top to bottom in red and green construction paper cutouts. Stars and reindeer and candy canes had been mangled together to form a backdrop. Before his stint as a temporary dad, Wyatt would've thought it ridiculous. Now that he knew just how much work kids like his nieces had put into the decor, he appreciated it for the fine art it was. He could only imagine how proud Dallas and Josie must be attending an event like this.

Mabel stood on his thighs, the heels of her tiny black patent dress shoes digging in. She was excited about seeing her "sissies" perform, which in her behavior manifested in much jumping and humming and lots of slobbery cheek kissing. "I *wuv* Unk Wy-att!"

He kissed her right back. "Love you, too, cutie."

"Mabel," Natalie said, "did you see the whole table filled with cookies we get to eat after the show?"

"Cookie! Cookie!" Jump, jump. Wyatt winced through the toddler's latest squeals.

The show began, and along with it, more emotional conflict than Wyatt was prepared to handle. All the kids were cute, but Bonnie and Betsy were off the charts. Through song after song, his mind drifted to the possibilities that would never be his. He would never sit in an audience, chest swelled with pride like the hundreds of parents around him. Odds were, he'd never even marry.

Surrounded by families and holiday cheer, he didn't just feel alone, but adrift.

Lord willing, he had fifty or so years left of life, but what would that time be filled with? Work? Meaningless hookups? Being the third wheel at every Buckhorn event? In giving up his Ethiopian gig, he'd been so sure he was making the right decision. Now, he wasn't.

Eyes stinging, he was glad for the dark. Glad for the

distraction of children singing over the growing sadness in his soul.

Natalie leaned close, whispering in his ear, "You okay?"

He nodded.

Hell no, he wasn't anywhere near okay. But his problems were his own, and not for Natalie's consumption.

By the time the show ended and the cookie and punch reception began, Wyatt pulled himself together. Tried focusing on the downside of kids. They were noisy and sticky and ran around screaming like atoms—not that he even knew if an atom made noise, but if it did, it had to be akin to hyper munchkins. So even knowing all of that, why was he still dissatisfied? As if everyone had been invited to join an exclusive club but him?

"All right," Natalie parked in front of him with a plastic cup of punch in one hand and a cookie in her other, "out with it. Why are you scowling? I'm sure there are a few hot single moms you could be hitting on."

A month earlier, Wyatt might've been tempted to cash in on that offer, but oddly enough, the only woman he was even remotely attracted to was Natalie. He'd grown fond of being around her. After their hospital visit Saturday, she'd remained strong while he'd been the one falling apart.

"Don't quote me on this," he said, striving for a teasing tone, "but I'm kind of crushing on you."

"Liar." Munching her cookie, she added, "You're just saying that to get out of giving Mabel her bath."

The little devil in question stood alongside her sisters, face wreathed in chocolate and red icing.

"You got me." Wyatt clutched his chest, glad for

the opportunity she'd unwittingly handed him to make light of his comment. What would she have said had she believed him? Might she have kissed him right here in front of God and all of Weed Gulch? "Where's Esther?"

Natalie nodded toward her friend Cami. The school secretary jiggled the grinning baby for a circle of cooing teachers. "She's a hot commodity."

"Excited for the day you're showing off your son?"

"Funny..." She finished her punch. "I haven't thought that far ahead. Right now, the logistics have me stymied."

"Like what? Anything I can do to help?"

"If you have a hankering to learn Lamaze. Or assemble the nursery furniture I have yet to buy. Or shop for diapers and onesies and—"

"Whoa." Hands on her shoulders, Wyatt gave her a comforting squeeze. "You still have a few months till the baby gets here, right?"

She nodded.

"All right, well, surely to God Josie will be home by then, and if she's not, your friend Cami would probably tackle Lamaze. As for the rest of it, just like the family has done for Christmas gifts—shop online. Once the stuff gets here, we can assemble after the kids are in bed."

"You'd do that for me?"

I'd do anything for you. The moment the thought popped in Wyatt's head, he knew to back off. That is, his head knew. As for his pulse... It raced full speed ahead.

"THANK YOU." IMMEDIATELY after opening her latest gift—a classroom decorating book from Natalie—Josie yawned. Still on morphine, it was plainly a struggle for her to remain awake.

"Dallas," Natalie said with forced Christmas cheer, "you're next." He nodded. Whereas Josie's head trauma issues had lessened to headaches, Dallas still had serious obstacles. His doctor said he'd make a full recovery, but for now, in addition to other problems, his speech was slurred. Dallas being Dallas, this frustrated him, which only exacerbated the situation and made him grumpy.

Georgina hustled to his side, helping him open a new fishing rod.

"Just had my lake stocked," Luke said. "By spring, I'll expect you to be out there with me."

Though the patients had been moved to a more homey long-term care facility, the fact remained that they were still celebrating Christmas in a sterile environment rather than at home. The tree Daisy had assembled was a crooked fake and because of Dallas's sensitivity to light, the only decorations were a few country-themed ornaments.

"I don't like it here," Bonnie announced midway through the next round of gifts. "It smells funny."

"Hush!" Georgina admonished. "With all your parents have been through, the last thing they need is to hear you complaining."

The girl's lower lip trembled in advance of full-blown tears. To her grandmother, she shouted, "You're mean!"

When Bonnie left the room, Betsy and Natalie followed.

"Hey," Natalie said, finally catching up with the runaway midway down the hall. Squeezing her in a hug, she barely held off her own waterworks. "Sweetheart, I know this is hard, but as much as you miss your mom and dad, they miss you. Seeing you helps them feel better."

"D-Daddy's weird," Betsy said, "and Mommy's always sleeping. And it *does* smell funny in there."

"I know." Natalie hugged them both. "But I promise everything will go back to normal soon. Your mom and dad and grandma will come home. Uncle Wyatt and I will go back to our own houses. Shoot, I'll bet by Valentine's Day, you'll forget any of this even happened."

"Really?" Bonnie asked, gazing up at Natalie through her big, blue eyes.

Nodding, Natalie said, "And until then, I need you to help with the little kids."

"I'll help," Betsy said.

"Me, too." Wyatt startled Natalie by joining their group hug. "It's going to take a lot of work to get Mabel to stop eating Play-Doh."

Bonnie giggled and sniffled. "She doesn't do that anymore."

"Does, too," Betsy said. "Kitty does, too. Then his poop's all blue and pink."

"Mmm, delightful." Natalie forced a smile. That answered her questions about the funky litter box contents.

"Quite a family we've got here, huh?" Natalie knew Wyatt had meant his words as a joke, but the knot in her throat told a different story. That, yes, in only a month, they had formed a family. Loud and messy and far from perfect, but a family all the same.

BARE FEET PROPPED ON THE coffee table, Wyatt asked Natalie, "Am I a bad person for feeling grateful Christmas is almost over?"

She laughed. "I was just thinking the same, so guess we'll be bad together."

"I like the sound of that." With a playful growl, he tugged her closer to his spot on the sofa. Aside from dancing firelight, the tree's colorful glow provided the room's only other illumination. There was no music. No TV. No crying or fighting kids. The pine tree's fresh scent provided a welcome change from the stuffy hospital. "You look pretty."

"You need glasses."

"Don't," he said, tucking flyaway hair behind her ears.

"What?"

"Berate yourself. You're a beautiful woman." Not trusting himself to behave, he satisfied his craving to kiss her with a chaste peck to her forehead.

"Thank you." Looking down, then up, she said, "Gotta say, you're kind of a beautiful man."

"I usually strive for handsome, but after the day we've had," he teased, "I'll take what I can get."

After an eye roll, she rested her head against his shoulder. He liked having her lean on him for support.

"Ooh." She clutched her belly.

"Baby kick?"

"Apparently, he's not happy with what Santa brought for Christmas." Wincing, she said, "There he goes again."

Easing off the sofa and onto his knees in front of her, he lifted her red sweater only to encounter a white tank. He slid that up and the waistband of her maternity jeans down. When Wyatt bracketed her baby, kissing the spot where the little guy again visibly moved, he heard Natalie's swift intake of breath.

Not sure if that was good or bad, he kissed her again. And again. And then clothes got in his way.

Turning his attention to her lips, he kissed her until she groaned. Until she raked her fingers through the hair at the back of his head, urging him closer and deeper and driving him crazy with sexy mewing sounds.

"I want you so bad," he said on a brief break for air.

Nodding, she said, "Likewise, but remember? We promised each other no more of this?"

"But it's Christmas," he reasoned.

She stole another deep kiss and murmured, "Maybe we could go a little further. Like you taking off your shirt."

"Me?" Rocking back on his heels, he said, "I was thinking more along the lines of you. I swear your *girls* grow a cup size every day."

Her playful swat only encouraged him.

And then they both undressed each other, kissing and caressing and speaking through lingering touches and glances and breathy sighs.

"I want to make love to you," he said, sweeping the backs of his fingers down the sides of her full breasts. She shivered—not from cold, but sensation.

She nodded, then shook her head. "We can't. I'm sorry. We just can't." Gathering her sweater and tank, she clutched them to her, rising from the sofa only to hurry up the stairs.

IN HER ROOM, NATALIE shut the door, leaning against it. The cold wood bit her bare back, reminding her just how close she and Wyatt had come to making love. For a woman determined to steer clear of all men—especially Wyatt—how was it that each day she grew closer to the one man above all she knew lacked a commitment gene. Sure, he might've backed out on his African adventure, but that didn't mean he didn't have another trip already planned.

In bed, she tossed and turned, alternately hoping Wyatt would come to her and praying he didn't.

When she woke in the morning to cold rain beating her windows, the empty side of her bed equally as chilly, she knew her prayer had come true. But she wasn't the least bit happy about it.

Then it dawned on her that for the first time since she'd started serving as a substitute mom for Josie, she'd slept through the night. She'd been so ashamed of her own actions with Wyatt that she'd run off without the baby monitor she'd left on the coffee table.

Bolting from bed, she ran to the nursery, fully expecting to find poor Esther soaked and screaming from hunger.

Instead, she found the baby's crib empty.

Racing down the hall and back staircase, she reached the kitchen only to freeze on the bottom step. The twins and Mabel sat at the kitchen table, eating scrambled eggs. Esther grinned in Wyatt's arms as he teased her with a teething ring.

"Good morning." He glanced up, making her pulse race from not only his gorgeous smile, but the charming scene.

"Why didn't you wake me?" She circled the table with kisses for all the girls.

"We're letting you rest!" Betsy hopped up to pull out the empty chair alongside her. In the process, three of the crayons she'd been using rolled onto the floor. "I made you a picture!" The scene she proudly displayed left a sentimental knot in Natalie's throat. "It's us four girls and you and Uncle Wyatt. We're a family!"

"And look!" Bonnie was also up, but she ran to the counter. "Us and Uncle Wyatt made you stuff to eat with lots of cheese!"

"Thank you." As Bonnie set a simple plate of eggs, bacon, strawberries and biscuits in front of her, Natalie was overcome with emotion.

"Here's honey for your biscuit." Betsy took the honey bear from Mabel to set it in front of Natalie.

Mabel screamed.

Natalie grimaced, making quick work of splitting her baked goods and drizzling them with honey. "This is so sweet of all of you," she said once Mabel had custody of her bear again. "Especially you." Gaze locked with Wyatt's, she feared all the air had vanished from the room. Just looking at him made her pulse quicken. Remembering what they'd almost shared made her cheeks flush.

"You're welcome," he said with a flirty wink. "You had a late night. Thought you and your baby could use the rest."

She shot him a scowl. "Had you left out the wink, I wouldn't now suspect your motive."

"How did we get from cheesy eggs to motive?"

His meal was too delicious to waste arguing. "Let's just say if you think wooing me through my stomach will produce results different from those we shared last night, you'd be wrong."

Eyebrows raised, he asked, "What if all I want are the same results?"

"You're incorrigible." The heat pouring from her cheeks rivaled the bacon's sizzle.

"Yep." He shifted a now dozing Esther to his other

shoulder. The sight of the baby lying safe in Wyatt's big, strong arms was mesmerizing. Natalie couldn't get over his transformation from professional bachelor to temporary dad. Esther's current contentment level meant he'd even managed a late-night feeding and changing her diaper. "That's part of my charm."

Bonnie asked, "What are you guys talking about?"

"And why are you looking all funny at each other?" Betsy wanted to know.

Mabel upended the honey bear and sucked the contents straight into her sticky mouth.

"I DON'T WANNA HAIRCUT!" The day before New Year's Eve, Bonnie wriggled and bucked in the beautician's chair.

"She doesn't like getting her hair cut." Betsy sat prim and proper for her hair dresser.

Mabel sat with Wyatt and Esther in the waiting area. Apprehension showed in her tightly folded arms and frown. Wyatt had tried reading to her, but she was too concerned about her sister to pay attention to a dancing bear.

"Bonnie, please," Natalie reasoned. "Your grandma told me that your mom and dad will be home soon. When they do get back, do you want to look like a shaggy hair monster?"

"Yeah," Betsy said. "Don't you wanna be a movie star like me?"

Bonnie stuck out her tongue.

Holding Esther to him with his right arm, Wyatt took Mabel by his left. "Come on, squirt. Let's see how bad this is really going to be."

"No cut!" Mabel said, refusing to budge.

"What if I get my hair cut first?" he asked.

She answered with an angry shake of her head.

Grunting from the girl's surprising weight, he hefted her up, as well. *"Noooooooo!"*

"She's such a baby," Bonnie said with disdain.

To Bonnie, he said, "How about straightening up and telling your little sister getting her hair cut is no big deal."

"Is so," Bonnie insisted.

"Look at me, Mabel." Betsy made a few supermodel poses. "I *loooove* going to the beauty parlor."

"Me, too," Natalie said.

Wyatt asked, "When's the last time you treated yourself to a fancy new 'do?"

"Can't remember." Facing the mirror, she asked, "Are you hinting I need womanly maintenance?"

"Not at all. Just thinking you might be the perfect person to show Mabel, here, that getting gussied up for her daddy is a good thing."

"Don't do it, Miss Nat," Bonnie said with a shake of her head.

"Stay still," her beautician requested. "If you don't, I may cut you."

"See?" Bonnie said. "This *is* super dangerous."

Sighing, Natalie asked the receptionist, "Does anyone have room on their schedule for me?"

They did and she proved a good sport. After Natalie's hair was washed, she welcomed Mabel onto her lap. As the stylist worked scissors around Natalie's head, the little girl stared into the mirror with rapt interest.

Betsy asked Wyatt, "How come you're not getting your hair cut?"

He gave Esther a jiggle. "I like mine rugged."

"That's not fair," Natalie said.

Bonnie had refused to have her dripping hair styled and sat in the reception area pouting.

"Yeah, Uncle Wyatt!" Betsy was having her hair blown dry. "If you had handsome hair, maybe you and Miss Nat could go on a date!"

"You think?"

His niece and her stylist nodded.

"Ask her," Betsy urged, "ask her!"

"Miss Nat," he said in front of her chair, ignoring her blazing cheeks. He knew he was playing with fire, but with the sun shining and his brother and sister-in-law making great progress, Wyatt was in the mood to throw caution into a campfire. "What do you think? Would an act as dramatic as me getting a haircut convince you to go on an official date?"

Her frown was almost as big as Bonnie's. "I thought we weren't going to go *there*."

"Hmm," Natalie's stylist said, "from the sound of that I'm guessing you two have already dabbled in romance?"

"No," Natalie said.

"Not really," Wyatt said.

Bonnie chimed in with, "Uncle Wyatt put his hands on Miss Nat's butt!"

Chapter Eleven

Standing on her parents' front porch, with Esther bundled in her arms, the twins bickering and Wyatt wrangling Mabel who kept insisting she didn't want to wear any clothes, Natalie wished herself back to her former, sane life. The salon had been stressful enough. An impromptu dinner invitation from Opal and Bud probably wouldn't prove relaxing.

"Aw," Opal opened the door wearing her favorite pink apron and a supersized smile, "don't you all look pretty! I heard about your big day at the beauty parlor."

"My lady almost stabbed me to death," Bonnie said, barging into the house, removing her coat only to toss it on the floor.

"Hey," Wyatt scolded. "Pick that up and ask Mrs. Lewis where she'd like you to hang it."

"Yeah," Betsy said. Her stylist had given her Shirley Temple curls. Ever since, she'd been in princess mode. "Ladies *always* hang their coats."

Bonnie stuck out her tongue.

"We didn't know *you* were coming," Opal said to Wyatt.

"Hot!" Mabel plopped her behind onto the living room carpet, tugging at her shoes and white tights.

"You've got your hands full." Natalie's father, Bud, took the twins' coats. "Wyatt. Opal may not have been expecting you, but it's always good seeing you. It's been a while."

"Yessir, it has." The men shook hands. Natalie had been pleasantly surprised when Wyatt volunteered to accompany her. Though at times he exasperated, flustered and mesmerized, more often than not, he was becoming a true friend.

The house was an old-fashioned ranch, featuring formal living and dining rooms and a big country kitchen. It had mostly beige decor, so the tall, dark-suited man seated on her mom's "fancy" sofa stood out like a lone orange-garbed OSU fan at an OU game.

"Honey," Opal practically dragged Natalie across the room. "I'd like you to meet my friend Alice's pride and joy, Ian. He just returned from Iraq and isn't sure whether to start a ranch or pursue something else. Either way, I knew *you'd* want to meet him." To Wyatt she said, "I appreciate you dropping off Natalie and the girls, but if you have things to do, we'll understand if you can't stay for dinner."

Wyatt waved off her concern, extending his hand to Ian, "Good to meet you. Thanks for serving."

Ian nodded. "Glad to meet both of you."

With Mabel still stripping, the older girls came over to investigate the new guy. "I'm Bonnie and this is my twin, Betsy. She looks just like me. 'Cause we're twins."

"That's cool," Ian said. "I'm glad to meet you, too."

"I just had my hairs decorated," Betsy said, fluffing her curls. "I'm gorgeous. But Bonnie didn't get her hairs done, so she's ugly."

"Am not!" Bonnie roared. "You're the ugly one."

"Oh my." Fingering her pearls, Opal said, "Girls, would you like to watch TV in the den?"

"No, thank you." Betsy checked herself out in the mirror hanging behind the sofa. "I want everyone to see how pretty I am."

"I'm *nekked*!" Mabel had finally gotten her way and ran, laughing and waving her arms, wearing nothing but the big red bow in her hair. *"Nekked! Nekked!"*

The night went downhill from there.

During dinner, Esther pitched the mother of all infant fits. Mabel put corn up her nose and Bonnie declared herself on a hunger strike. Betsy announced she was on a movie star diet and ate only mashed potatoes.

By dessert and after-dinner coffee, Esther had thankfully fallen asleep in her carrier and the twins took Mabel to watch TV.

"Whew," Bud said, sipping at his French roast, "those girls are quite a handful. Natalie, bet it makes you glad for having a man around the house—even if Wyatt is only temporary."

Natalie swallowed a groan.

Opal cleared her throat. "Ian told me he once volunteered to coach his base's Little League team. He's very good with children. In fact, his mom told me he won an award for his charitable activities."

Looking as if he'd like to crawl beneath the table, Ian said, "It wasn't a big deal."

"Sure was," Bud added, "he even won a plaque."

Their guest ducked behind his coffee cup. "Since it's getting late, I should probably go."

"Already?" Opal complained. "At least let me get you a piece of pie to take home. Your mother has been hounding me for my recipe for years, but it's a family secret. Natalie knows my banana cream recipe, though.

Don't you, honey? My Natalie is a very accomplished cook."

Forcing a smile, Natalie said, "Ian, it was a pleasure meeting you. Good luck in whatever career path you choose."

"Thanks." The poor guy looked as put off by her mother's transparent matchmaking technique as Natalie had been. "Wyatt, I might give you call about my folks' abandoned wells. With oil prices so high, might be worth the cost to reopen a few."

Wyatt withdrew his wallet, offering Ian a business card. "Anytime."

With Ian out of the house, Opal attacked. "Honey, isn't he handsome? And so accomplished. When I heard you'd just gotten your hair done, I knew this was the perfect night for you two to meet. Although I didn't expect Wyatt to tag along."

Natalie stood, stacking dessert plates to take to the kitchen.

Bud said, "Honey, don't be upset with your mom. Time is ticking for you to find a father for your baby."

As if to remind them he was still in the room, Wyatt cleared his throat.

"Damn it." Fuming, Natalie slammed the dishes in the sink with enough force to snap the bottom two. "For the last time, I'm fine raising this baby on my own. Craig's leaving was horrible. Why would I ever put myself—let alone my child—in the position of being walked out on again? Because trust me, even if I did suddenly find a husband, what's to stop him from leaving? What man in his right mind would even want to father another man's baby?"

Opal began to cry.

Of course, Bud put his arms around her.

Who comforted poor, pregnant Natalie? No one.

"THAT WAS QUITE A tongue-lashing you gave your folks." Long after they'd put the girls to bed, Wyatt found Natalie nursing a cup of her favorite mint tea.

She shrugged.

"You really feel that way? Like just because you're pregnant, you're damaged goods?"

Sipping her tea, she asked, "Any chance of you leaving me alone? Because I'm pretty sure you once said the same."

In response, he hefted himself onto the counter, pillaging the contents of the cookie jar. "It's not really my business, but Nat, you're an amazing woman—inside and out. Any man would be lucky to have you and your son."

Any man, but not you. As soon as the thought hit her head, Natalie fought to erase it. What had happened to her to go from hating Wyatt to considering him to be one of her closest friends? Possibly even more? What would happen when Dallas and Josie returned home, ending the cozy family scenario she and Wyatt had formed? "Please, leave me alone."

"No can do." Hopping off the counter, he joined her at the table. "Wanna take a walk?"

"Love to, but we can't leave the girls alone."

He thumped his forehead. "Rookie new-dad mistake."

"But you're not a dad."

Once her statement sunk in, his smile faded.

"As soon as Dallas and Josie return, we're out of here. The dumbest thing you ever did was not going to Africa. You could've had a fresh start. A clean slate. Isn't that what you want?"

"Yeah, Nat. You nailed it."

She moved to freshen her tea.

"Is there any subject you won't overanalyze?"

She poured steaming water from the teapot into her mug, then dunked her tea bag. "Is there any analysis you won't question?"

"WHAT ARE YOU DOING?" Wyatt woke the morning of New Year's Eve to find all hell breaking loose in the kitchen. At 5:00 a.m., not even the kids were out of bed, so what was a barn-big pregnant woman doing on a rickety stepladder? "Seriously, you need to get down from there."

"Don't tell me what to—" She turned too fast, in the process losing her balance.

He caught her in time to avoid major damage, but not fast enough to save her ankle from twisting.

Natalie winced, grabbing his T-shirt for support. "Ouch."

A roll of paper towels fell from the niche above the cabinets, bouncing off the counter to hit the floor.

"Out with it. Why on God's green earth were you up there cleaning?"

"Your mom's going to be home soon. I don't want her thinking I haven't properly cared for her beautiful house." She made a motion for the towels, but her ankle wasn't having it.

"Sit," he requested.

For once in her stubborn life, she did as he asked. A quick inspection showed some swelling and what he guessed was a minor sprain.

"How is it?" It hadn't occurred to him, but from her

current awkward angle, she couldn't see her ankle past her belly.

"You'll live, but probably need extra rest."

"No time." She pushed up, only to have him urging her back down. "Wyatt, seriously. Josie's due to be released any day. Dallas in a week. Even though Georgina will no doubt hire round-the-clock nurses to help, she won't have time to do the basics. Plus, the patients need an ultraclean environment for—"

"Are you aware you're rambling and sound loopy?"

"You're an ass."

He pulled around the chair opposite hers, propped her leg on it. "I've been called worse. You're not nesting, are you? Because I read about it in that pregnant lady book of yours, and if you are—nesting—it's too early."

Eyebrows raised, she asked, "You've been reading *What to Expect When You're Expecting?*"

"You don't have to look so shocked. I figure as long as we're stuck together, I need to know the score. Just in case."

For the longest time she sat staring, then burst out laughing. "And you call me crazy?"

"Because I care?"

"Why? You have no stake in this baby. Odds are, just as soon as Dallas and Josie get home, the two of us will go back to seeing each other only on special occasions." Hands protectively over her belly, her eyes shone with unshed tears.

How did he begin to explain that the more he was around her, the more he wanted a *stake* in her baby. He had no rational reasoning. Nothing but a vague sense that when it came to Natalie and her son, he didn't want to miss a thing. Wyatt wanted to be a friend to her, a mentor to her kid. Only how did he do all that when he had no right?

Fate had been pretty clear about the fact that he shouldn't be a father. It didn't matter that during his time with his nieces, he'd not only enjoyed himself, but had done a good job co-parenting. From the start, he'd known this job would end. As for being a full-time dad, Wyatt knew literally and figuratively he didn't have it in him. But Lord, how he at least wanted the chance to try.

Forcing a deep breath, he said, "Cash called last night."

"What'd he want?"

"He told me Wren isn't working tonight, but her idea of a celebration is to stay home, lounging in front of their TV. Cash wanted to know if we'd like a night off. If so, they'll watch all of our girls."

"*All* of them?" Eyes wide, she asked, "Even wicked little Bonnie?"

He laughed. "I know, I was shocked, too. But hell, I figure if they're dumb enough to offer, we should be smart enough to take them up on it." Giving her shoulders a light massage, he asked, "Well? What do you think?"

She nodded.

WITH HER CHARGES GONE, Natalie took her time getting ready. She lounged forever in her bathroom's deep tub, then squeezed herself into one of Josie's sequined maternity gowns. She curled her hair, sweeping a portion up, letting the rest fall in soft curls.

In the kitchen that morning, Wyatt had been right. She had succumbed to temporary insanity. More than anything in the world, she wanted to spend the last night of the year acting as carefree as Wyatt's kisses made her feel.

After all, what was the worst that could happen? She was already pregnant.

An hour later, Wyatt had transported her to Grange Hall's annual New Year's Eve party. She'd been to a half-dozen or more, but never had she seen the old place look more festive. Tiny white lights had been strung from the rafters, and black, white and silver balloons provided sophistication to the homespun buffet comprised of potluck classics.

"We forgot to bring a dish," she said, wishing her ankle wasn't throbbing. It didn't help that the heels she'd borrowed from Josie were a half-size too small. What did help was holding on to Wyatt's strong arm.

"The case of champagne out in the truck is our dish. I wanted to get you settled before bringing it in."

"I can't drink champagne." Which was sad, because she loved it.

"That's why I also grabbed a case of sparkling cider for teetotalers like you." He guided her to the nearest black-clothed table. "Be all right here until I get back?"

"Fine."

Upon his return, in between servings of hash-brown casserole and beef stew, laughing with old friends and explaining too many times that not only were they not a couple, but Wyatt wasn't her baby's father, Natalie was tired, but almost glad for the few awkward turns the night had taken. Had it been too perfect, she might've let down her guard, daring to hope for more from Wyatt than this one, special evening.

"I've wanted to dance with you for hours," he said, holding her in his arms beneath a shimmering disco ball. Swaying to a slow song, she forgot her ankle hurt and remembered the sensation of falling in love. Only she wasn't fooling herself by believing for a second that's what was happening. She and Wyatt had shared a lot, but love would never be theirs. "I think I already told you, but in case I haven't, you look amazing."

"Thank you." Smiling up at him, she said, "You're looking awfully spiffy in your suit."

"I want to kiss you."

Then why don't you? Mouth dry, she forgot to breathe.

"But after we've told all these fine folks how we're just friends, I suppose we should behave."

Aren't you the one always urging me to be bad? "You're right."

"But when the clock strikes twelve…well," he chuckled. "It wouldn't be right ringing in the new year without a proper kiss."

"I agree."

Once the countdown started, they gravitated closer and closer. The crowd vanished. All Natalie remembered was her hunger for this man's lips to graze hers.

Three…

Closer.

Two…

Closer.

By mutual unspoken agreement, they skipped *one* and went straight to their own personal celebration.

Chapter Twelve

"You passed the house."

"I know," Wyatt said, turning onto his own drive.

"I miss my own home. I want to be there with you."

Instead of speaking, she reached for his hand.

Easing his fingers between hers, he knew the night would be unforgettable. He hoped in a good way.

His glass house reflected the dark forest. He'd chosen the tinted material for its reflective quality. In subtle ways, it was a lot like him. He enjoyed looking out, but preferred no one looking in. For if his personal life was inspected too closely, it would be all too possible to see his flaws.

Barely an hour into the month, January was proving brutal.

Wyatt hustled Natalie inside, pointing her toward the restroom while he turned up the central heat and made a fire.

"This place is breathtaking," she said. Having taken off her heels, she'd startled him. "See many deer or other animals?"

"All the time. Raccoon. Coyote. Opossum." He added another log to the fire. "Before he was married,

Cash stayed out here once and told me he saw a bear, but you know Cash and his love for a good tall tale."

"Cash?" Grinning, Natalie stood next to Wyatt in front of the fire. "Can't imagine him spinning a yarn."

"Want tea? Might not be your favorite flavor, but I'm sure I can scrounge up—"

Placing her fingers over his lips, she said, "Enough small talk. You and I are both adults and no matter how much we'd like to pretend we don't know where this night is going, we do."

Hands low on her hips, he asked, "What about everything you said last night? You know I have nothing long-term to offer."

"And you know I'm determined to raise my baby on my own." Arching her head back, she pulled pins from her long hair, sending it in a wild tumble.

"I'm trying not to be that guy, Nat. I don't want to use a pregnant woman for sex."

Lips pressed tight, she shook her head. "You're telling me now's the time you decide to grow a conscience?"

"I don't want to per se, but should."

Raspy, as if not sure where to find her next breath, she asked, "Where's that leave us? Other than in your amazing house. Not a kid in sight—unless you count my baby bump." Natalie's voice was barely audible above the crackling fire. He'd been around the block more than a few times and usually picked up on a woman's hint to take things to an intimate level. But Natalie wasn't just any woman. He'd grown to care for her. Deeply. If they did make love, would he wake regretting it?

Worse, would she?

"Your son is very real." Tugging her to him, it took

his every ounce of willpower not to unzip her dress. "If we do what I'm pretty sure you're suggesting, will we still be friends in the morning?"

"Since when do you care?" Natalie gave him a mighty shove, but he held firm.

"I've always cared. I have too much respect for you to use you."

"What if I'm using you?"

That threw him off balance. Now he was the one releasing her and backing away. "The Nat I know would never say something so crass."

"For the record, as soon as my baby's born, I'll never be the same. Christmas night, you wanted to take it further, but I said no. Why is it now a problem for *me* to want physical pleasure?"

Hands to his forehead, Wyatt said, "Nat, it's not a problem. We're consenting adults. The thing is, just last night you were adamant we not make love, now you're—"

"Don't you ever shut up?" Bridging the gap between them, she tossed her arms around his neck, kissing him with passion he didn't even try to deny.

Her lips still pressed to his, she removed his suit coat and loosened his tie.

All night she'd tortured him with her dress. Josie wasn't nearly as blessed as Natalie in the boob department. Squeezed into the figure-skimming gown, Natalie's breasts had heaved and teased. Now, Wyatt didn't waste a second ditching the garment. But then she presented him with another dilemma—a black lace bra and thong that in dancing firelight proved the most erotic thing he'd ever seen.

"You're stunning," he managed before nuzzling her cleavage, moving down to her huge belly. He'd never been with a pregnant woman, and Natalie was proving a major turn-on. It no longer mattered another man was her baby's father. Wyatt blocked the fact from his mind, preferring to picture himself in that role. And why shouldn't he?

He dropped his pants and boxers, freed her breasts and helped her step clear of her thong. He sat on the sofa, aching with need. She sat astride him, easily taking him in, setting a rhythm seemingly calculated to cause him the most pleasure. Leaning forward, bracing herself on his shoulders, she covered his mouth with hers. Their tongues mimicked motions old as time. All too soon, he tensed before succumbing to a white-hot thrill. Natalie visibly trembled. Her internal quivers thrilled him anew.

Smiling, still breathing heavy, she asked, "Does this place have a tub?"

"Depends," he teased, "do I get to join you?"

"YOU BEING SUCH A take-charge woman is a turn-on."

Natalie splashed Wyatt with warm water. "In my current condition, unless we really wanted to get kinky, there wasn't much choice."

"Hmm…" His expression brightened. "Talk like that gives a man ideas."

Yawning, she said. "Too bad for you it's going to take days for me to regain the energy we just burned."

"I've got time." His flirty grin renewed her craving for more grown-up fun, but also saddened her to think they'd never be intimate again.

She'd allowed herself this one night, but no more. Any further close contact and Natalie might never let him go. Trouble was, he never wanted to be caught.

"YOU BOTH LOOK GREAT." A week later, Natalie jiggled Esther while the private nurse Georgina had hired took Josie's and then Dallas's vital signs.

"Thanks." Josie held out her hand for Natalie to hold. "How can I ever show you enough appreciation for all you've done?"

"Nothing but your full recovery is needed," Natalie said, voice hoarse with gratitude that her friends were finally well enough to return home. Truth be told, as much as Natalie had enjoyed her time playing house with Wyatt and the girls, Natalie should be thanking Josie.

The couples' king-size bed had been replaced with two rented hospital beds and a new shelf loaded with medical supplies had been set in place of Josie's giant weeping fig. Aside from those changes, the elegant room with its thick carpet and burgundy floral bedding and draperies remained the same. Even cheery sunlight warmed the dangerously cold day.

"Give me that baby," Dallas barked. Still wearing a cast and struggling with headaches, his grumpy-meter spiked off the charts.

"Yes, sir." Natalie gingerly handed him his daughter.

"Hello, gorgeous." Cradling the infant to his chest, he kissed the downy top of her head. "I was beginning to wonder if I'd ever hold you again."

"I never lost hope," Natalie said. How amazing would it be to have a man so much in love with her son?

Josie asked, "How long until the twins get home from school?"

Consulting her watch, Natalie said, "A couple hours.

Mabel's probably about done with her nap. Want me to get her?"

Josie turned down her offer. "She's always cranky when she has to wake before she's ready."

"True," Natalie said with an understanding laugh. It was a strange sensation, knowing her friends' children so well.

"I'll bet you're ready to get home," Dallas said.

"I suppose." Seated in a lounge chair, Natalie wasn't sure what to do with her hands. She'd spent so much time chasing after the girls that now that her help was no longer needed, she felt a little lost. The home she'd once found perfect would now seem shabby and cramped.

"With Georgina and the nurse here," Josie said, "please don't feel obligated to stay. I'm sure you're itching to get back to school. I know I am."

Was it wrong Natalie hadn't thought about returning to her once-fulfilling job?

Dallas said, "I can only imagine the mess Wyatt's made of my ranch. Sooner I get out on the range, the better."

"He's done great." Natalie recalled the afternoon after Wyatt had inspected for damage after the snow. Finding the dead cattle had been hard on him. "You owe him a big thank-you for working so hard to keep everything running just the way you like. Not only that, but he's helped me in caring for the girls."

"That was quite a speech," Josie noted. "Anything you want to tell me?"

Praying her superheated cheeks didn't give her away, Natalie snapped, "No. Wyatt and I are friends. Nothing more."

"They totally did the deed." Using his free hand, Dallas bunched the pillows beneath his head.

"You're horrible," Josie said to her husband. "Remind me why I married you?"

Over Esther's head, he blew her a kiss. "Because together, we make gorgeous babies."

"That's right," Josie said. "Looking at that angelic face, how could I forget?"

Five minutes of Dallas and Josie's lovey-dovey banter proved Natalie's limit.

In her room, she packed her few belongings, being extra careful not to crush the precious pictures drawn for her by Mabel, Betsy and Bonnie. Her favorite was a no-brainer—the one Betsy had given her, featuring all four girls and their temporary mommy and daddy. The one she'd proudly proclaimed was a representation of their family.

The family now officially disbanded.

Where was Wyatt? Josie and Georgina had tried calling his cell, but he hadn't answered. Not surprising considering some of the remote areas of the ranch he might've gone to. Would he care she was gone?

Knowing she wasn't strong enough to deal with her shattered emotions should he not, she hugged her friends and both their daughters. She found Georgina in the kitchen and hugged her, too.

At that point, self-preservation kicked in. Without making another stop, she all but ran to her car.

LOWERING THE BRIM OF HIS cowboy hat, Wyatt shaded his eyes from the sun. Astride his favorite paint, Oreo, Wyatt caught a flash of chrome. Where was Natalie headed this time of day?

A glance at his watch had him wondering if there was something wrong with one of the twins.

He kicked Oreo into a gallop, making it from the high pasture to the house in record time. If something was wrong, Natalie would have at least left him a note.

After reining his horse to the hitching post near the back door, he headed inside. Damn if his pulse wasn't racing from apprehension. If the twins were all right, what if something had happened to Esther or Mabel? Worse yet, Natalie's unborn son?

Wyatt was midway through searching the kitchen when laughter floated from upstairs.

Tackling the back stairs two at a time, he jogged the hall only to get a shock. Settled pretty as you please in the master bedroom were Dallas and Josie. Josie held Esther while Dallas worked the TV remote. Mabel sat on Georgina's lap. A uniformed nurse stood in a slant of sun, writing on what looked to be a chart.

All Wyatt could think to say was, "Where's Nat? She okay?"

"Nice to see you, too," Dallas said in his customary gruff tone.

"I didn't think y'all were getting in till later. Nat's making her special meat loaf for dinner."

"Already did," Georgina said, braiding Mabel's hair. "She left it in the fridge. Such a sweet girl. Too bad she can't find a husband."

"She doesn't want one," Wyatt snapped.

"Trust me, every girl wants one." Putting a bow on the end of one braid, Georgina started on the other side.

"No," he fired back, "Nat told me that after Craig left, she'll never trust another guy. She's afraid of getting hurt."

"Hmph." Georgina didn't look convinced.

Josie said, "Sounds like you two got to know each other fairly well."

Wyatt shrugged. "I s'pose. Anyway, where is she?"

"Naturally," Georgina said, "she went home."

"Just like that? She didn't even say goodbye?"

"Sure, she did." Josie kissed her baby. "Just not to you."

For the life of him, Wyatt couldn't figure why he cared, but Natalie taking off without so much as a backward glance in his direction incensed him. Had what they shared—whatever it happened to be—meant so little?

"Wyatt, sweetie," Josie said, "would you mind doing me a huge favor and changing Esther's diaper? She smells suspicious."

Dallas asked, "Since when does my little brother change diapers?"

"Natalie taught him." Wyatt loved how Josie and his brother discussed him as though he was a trained circus pony.

"Come here," he said to a fussing Esther. Cradled to his chest, she quieted.

"She likes you," Josie noted. "I'm glad you two finally bonded."

"Hell," Dallas said with a laugh, "we should send him a bill for all the parenting experience we gave him. By the time he has his own kids, he'll already be a pro."

Wyatt wanted to hold in his frustration for a time when he and Dallas were alone, really, he did, but his temper got the best of him. "You know, Dallas, when it comes to you and your one-liners, I can't take one more. For the record, I will never have kids. So each and every time you aim a dig at me for not being married with rug rats of my own, you twist the dagger deeper."

"Wh-what?" Georgina was instantly by his side. "Why are you saying this? How would you even know?"

He gave them the abridged version, after which, though the ladies present coated him with sympathy and apologies for times they said things that they now realized were insensitive, Dallas remained stoic.

"Aren't you going to say anything?" Wyatt finally spouted.

"Only thing that comes to mind is sorry." Dallas's expression was solemn. "I've been so hard on you, because more than anything, for Dad's memory, I wanted to be surrounded by so many Buckhorns I never missed Dad again, but I should've known something was up with you. You haven't been yourself, have you? That why we spend more time bickering than getting along the way brothers should?"

"I guess," Wyatt said with a shrug. "You just have this way of saying things that cut to the core—especially on this issue. I'm tired of it. Even if I could have kids, would it be any of your business when I chose to bring them into the world?"

"No, man. It wouldn't. I'm sorry." Dallas held out his arms for a hug, and, not sure where he might still be bruised, Wyatt gingerly accepted.

Once Esther was changed, Wyatt carried her into Natalie's room. Was it his imagination, or was the air flavored with her light floral perfume?

He sat hard on the foot of the bed.

Eyes closed, it was all too easy to relive New Year's Eve. Beyond that, the hot kisses they'd shared in here.

He, more than anyone, knew they'd never be more

than friends, but didn't even friends give each other a courtesy goodbye? Why did he feel as if she'd taken part of him with her? The best part.

"Esther," he whispered into the infant's downy hair, "how did I let myself get in this deep? I *really* like Miss Nat. She's smart and funny and sexy as sin. Why didn't you warn me to stay away?"

Unfortunately, Wyatt's niece chose drooling over doling out advice.

"STILL OVERWHELMED?" On a breather from the school's usual morning rush of calls and parents barraging the front desk, Cami popped into Natalie's office.

"More like drowning." Dropping her head to her desk, Natalie said, "The mail alone is too much. Throw in all the paperwork long past due and calls needing to be made and I might catch up by Easter." She'd been back two days, but didn't feel remotely in her groove.

Her mornings spent around the big Buckhorn family table with Wyatt and the girls felt like a dream. She'd stopped by Bonnie and Betsy's classroom for hugs from them, but what about Mabel and Esther? Did they miss her? What about Wyatt? Had she been nothing but a diversion to him?

"I know that weepy look," Cami said. "Please tell me the rumors I've heard about you and Wyatt hooking up aren't true."

Natalie wanted to reassure her friend. Tell her no way would she be foolish enough to succumb to Wyatt's charm. She wanted to do that, but how could she without lying?

"Oh, no…" Sitting on the sofa, Cami asked, "How serious are you? Dating or just fooling around?"

"Stop." Focusing on the nearest pile of mail needing

to be sorted, Natalie said, "What happened between us was no biggee. A few kisses and—"

"Were they hot?"

Natalie covered her flaming face with a supply catalog.

"Yes?" Off the sofa, Cami snatched Natalie's catalog. "Oh my gosh—details. *Now.*"

Where to start? At first, yes, the kisses she'd shared with Wyatt had been plenty steamy. But the more time they spent together, the more experiences they'd shared, the more everything changed. She'd felt an inexplicable connection to him. At least she thought she had. Having not spoken to him since the morning she left, she now knew their kisses and lovemaking were no more real than Santa. But if that were true, why did she miss him so badly? Their late-night conversations? His laugh? The feeling she wasn't alone?

Cami whistled. "Judging by your silence, you've got it bad. What are you going to do?"

"The only thing I can. For now, immerse myself in work. Then, once my baby comes, I'll be so busy caring for him, I'll forget Wyatt Buckhorn exists."

Chapter Thirteen

By early February, Wyatt wished he could say he no longer thought about Nat, but the truth was he didn't just miss her, he needed her so badly her absence in his life was like a physical ache. How selfish would he have been, though, to further immerse himself into her life, knowing full well he had nothing to offer?

This explained why he was now freezing his ass off in Deadhorse, Alaska. A few days after his talk with his family, one of Wyatt's best welders had walked off the site, and Wyatt had jumped at the chance to fill in for him until finding someone else.

As a general rule, when life turned rocky, hard labor served as his lifeline. Up here, there was nothing to do other than work, eat and sleep. As the "boss," his men didn't understand his penchant for getting his hands dirty. Wyatt didn't understand, either, but what could it hurt?

Being back in Weed Gulch? Stuck behind his desk with only a stack of paperwork keeping him from Natalie and her huge belly? That would bring about true pain.

After twelve-hour days working rig maintenance

in temperatures of thirty-five below, sleep came easy. Forgetting his night with Natalie? Not so much.

A WEEK BEFORE VALENTINE'S Day, Natalie knocked on Principal Moody's office door.

"If you're over five feet tall," the iron-haired woman shouted, "enter!"

Natalie grinned. "I qualify, but barely."

"I presume Cami told you I need a favor?"

Helping herself to one of the guest chairs, Natalie said, "As long as I can sit through the task, my swollen feet will be happy to help."

"Good." She opened a file folder, read a sticky note and tossed it in the trash. "Got a call this morning from the president of the high school's PTA and they are desperate for chaperones for Saturday night's dance. Think you can help?"

The prospect wasn't appealing, but so many of Natalie's friends and coworkers had done favors for her when she'd taken leave to watch Josie's girls, that it would've been bad for her karma to now turn someone down.

Forcing a smile, Natalie said, "I'd love to."

"Excellent. Be at the high school gymnasium by six-thirty, dressed in formal attire. Or," she added with a chuckle, "whatever you comfortably fit into."

"Was that a dig at my nonexistent waistline?"

"Not at all, dear. Just *keepin' it real,* as our students would say. Oh—and along those same lines, please feel free to bring a date. I've promised your mom I'd try to get you married."

The only thing saving the principal from getting a piece of Natalie's mind was her ringing office phone.

"HOW ABOUT THIS ONE?" It took a while, but Josie walked the entire length of her closet to show off a stretchy black gown, featuring white crystals around the collar and cuffs. "I wore it to one of Georgina's parties nine months pregnant with Mabel."

"It's gorgeous," Natalie said, "but the sight of you walking without any help is even better."

"Aw, thanks." Josie walked an extra five feet to give Natalie a hug.

Natalie teased, "Now you're just showing off."

She winced. "And I'm feeling it. Come lounge with me."

With Dallas out of his cast, the couples' king-size bed was back. "When I picked up the girls from school yesterday, Cami asked if you'd found a date for the dance."

"Cami has a big mouth."

"Granted," Josie said with a smile, "but for the record, Wyatt found a replacement welder sooner than he'd expected, and now he's home."

Abruptly sitting up, Natalie asked, "What do you mean, home? Where's he been?"

"Doing whatever oil thing he does in Alaska." She took a movie magazine from her nightstand. "Poor guy looks like hell. His skin is all chapped and windburned. He could use serious TLC." Flashing a picture of a starlet in a crimson gown, she asked, "What do you think of this for me to wear for V-Day? Dallas hired a limo to drive us to a huge party at Southern Hills Country Club."

Natalie ignored her friend and muttered, "Who in his right mind goes to Alaska in February?"

"Forget Wyatt." Josie wagged her magazine. "If I'm

going to get this dress in time, I'll have to order it to-night."

"It's amazing. But does Wyatt need help? Has he been eating right?"

Eyes narrowed, Josie asked, "For a woman who claims to only be *pals* with my brother-in-law, what's up with all the questions?"

Trying to play it cool, Natalie shrugged. "I'm a counselor. I get paid to care."

"For children, Nat. Not Wyatt."

"Whatever." Pulse racing, Natalie scooped up the dress Josie was loaning her. "I have a lot to do. You and Dallas have fun on your big night out."

By the time Natalie reached her car, she had to remind herself to breathe. The news that Wyatt had been off in the middle of nowhere rather than pur-posely ignoring her provided a tremendous boost to her mood.

He's just a friend, she told herself on the way down his drive. After a long absence, she'd be excited to see anyone she hadn't visited in a while.

Even so, she pressed harder on the gas. What if he wasn't home? What if he was? Why the hurry to get to him when she didn't know what to say?

Her belly was huge. Skin blotchy. Hair a squirrel-tail mess. Knowing Wyatt, he'd attend the dance with her out of good, old-fashioned pity.

Slamming on the brakes, she stopped the car in the center of the blacktop lane. What was she doing?

Her logical side screamed for her to turn back now. She'd already worked past the roughest part of being without Wyatt. Meanwhile, her hormone-driven emo-tions dared her forward. The affection Wyatt had shown her New Year's Eve hadn't been imagined. He did care for her. But to what extent?

"LOOK AT YOU!" FROM HIS home office, Wyatt had seen Natalie pull up. Ever since hitting town, he'd wanted to call, but hadn't known what to say. Having thrown open the front door, he jogged down the few steps, wrapping her in a hug. "You don't have a baby in there, but a water buffalo."

"A what?" she said with a hoarse laugh.

"I don't know. It was the only thing I could think of on the fly." Taking her hands, he stepped back for a better view. "You're stunning."

"You need glasses." Flushed from his compliment, she bowed her head.

There were so many things he wanted to ask. Why she'd left without saying goodbye. Whether or not she'd missed him. If she'd thought about their night together as many times as him.

"Come in," he said, ushering her through the door. "It's cold. I'll build a fire."

"Don't go to any trouble."

"I'm not. Just making sure my friend is comfortable and warm." Lord, he was acting like the biggest girl-crazy nerd in high school. Lately, Natalie had this affect on him, but no matter what, he wouldn't let their reunion get out of control. When it came to mutual chemistry, there was no question they had it. But that didn't give him the green light to kiss her, make love to her, wish himself whole to be worthy of her. "Look at your poor ankles."

"Don't remind me. My feet have been replaced by bricks."

He guided her to the sofa, helped her lie down. He

took off her shoes and raised her sock-covered feet. From his football-playing days he recalled elevating swollen limbs, so he took a pillow from the opposite couch and lifted her feet onto that. "Better?"

"Heaven," she said with what he remembered as her contented smile.

"Want tea?" His brain told him to stop hovering. Runaway pulse said to do whatever it took to keep her happy in his home.

"You're spoiling me."

"That's kind of the plan." By the time the fire crackled, radiating heat, the water was boiling for her tea. He dunked the bag until the coloring was right. To satisfy her sweet tooth, he scooped in plenty of sugar.

Once she cradled her steaming mug, she said, "Thanks. I didn't come here to be waited on, but a girl could get used to this kind of service."

"Why are you here?" he blurted. "Not that I'm complaining, but no one even knows I'm in town."

"Josie told me."

"Good." Was it wrong that he'd hoped his sister-in-law would have news about Natalie? Each time he'd brought up her friend, Josie had changed the subject. Maddening. He'd left the main house kicking himself for not having gone straight home. Had she known what she was doing all along?

"I was over there to borrow a dress. My principal asked me to chaperone the high school dance, and since we're guilty of practically every punishable offense the kids might try to pull, I wondered if you'd like to go with me—not as a date, or anything—just as friends."

Wyatt's mood plummeted.

The F word brought on a headache. Logic dictated

friends were all they would ever be, but part of him craved more. And that made him sad. Resigned.

"Sounds fun," he said, forcing a carefree tone.

"I think so." Her exhale was exaggerated and slow. Had she feared he'd turn her down? "It's formal. You have a tux, right?"

"Sure." Didn't every dedicated bachelor?

"What's wrong?" Natalie asked. "You look upset."

"Tired." Tired of missing her. Craving her. Wondering what it would feel like to cradle her newborn son.

"LADIES," NATALIE SAID to the group of teen girls dumping the contents of a flask of rum into the punch, "let's have a chat with the principal."

After escorting the threesome to the equivalent of high school jail, Natalie rejoined Wyatt at their table. Techno music blaring, she didn't know what she'd been thinking in hoping the night held romance. At this point, her feet and head throbbed and escape had become her top priority.

"Gorgeous and powerful," Wyatt teased, standing to draw out her chair. "Lethal combination."

"Watch it," she warned, "I'll toss you in detention, too."

He ate a few corn chips. "That's all they get for booze?"

"Actually, the boozers will get suspended. Detention's reserved for dress code violations and folks trying to sneak in without tickets."

"At least I'll be in good company." He grinned, but Natalie wasn't feeling it.

The whole night had been *off.* Her hair refused to cooperate and her feet were so swollen the only one dancing was her baby—directly on top of her bladder. She'd spent more time in the bathroom than in the gym.

"Tired?"

She nodded.

"How long do you have to stay?"

"Until eleven." Rubbing the back of her neck, she said, "Wonder if they'd mind me sneaking out early."

"You're not having the baby, are you?" Concern marred his handsome features.

"No. I've got a little over a month before he's due."

Wyatt started in on the plastic bowl of M&M's. "Guess I'm still scarred from when Wren had Robin midway through her and Cash's wedding reception."

"I heard that was quite a night." Techno was replaced by a country ballad.

"Feel up to a dance?" He held out his hand. Part of her wanted to take him up on his offer, but gazing across the wood floor at a sea of couples reminded her how pointless welcoming Wyatt back into her life would be. He wasn't marriage material and she wasn't in any position to take emotional chances.

"I hate to do this here," she said, "but I made a mistake in asking you here tonight."

"Where is this coming from?" Leaning forward, he asked, "Did I do something to offend you?"

Where did she start? Only how could she be offended by the core of who Wyatt was? He'd never misrepresented himself by claiming to be anyone other than the bachelor he'd chosen to be. In the same vein, how many times had she told him she was determined to be a single mom?

"Because if so," he continued, "give me a chance to make things right."

"Ever asked yourself why we're attracted to each other?"

His grin adorable, he suggested, "'Cause we're both damned good-looking?"

"Wyatt, I'm serious. The only reason we're constantly hot for each other is the whole forbidden thrill factor. It's just like these kids. If they were told it's perfectly all right for them to attend the dance in dresses that look more like lingerie, do you think they'd still want to do it? You and I both know we're wrong for each other. *If* I ever fall for another man, he needs to be a natural-born father. A rock. The kind of guy who sticks around through good times and bad. Like Cash or Dallas or Luke." *Wait,* her conscience screamed. *Didn't Wyatt cancel his trip multiple times to stay with his nieces and her?* Yes, she fought back, but that didn't mean he'd been satisfied with his decision. It was one thing choosing to do something of free will. Another if you complete a task purely out of a sense of duty. Taking his hands, she said, "Wyatt, you're a lot of fun, and lately you've proven yourself great with kids, but to the best of my knowledge, you've never been with the same woman for over two months. With my baby nearly here, I can't afford to fall for you, only to have you break my heart."

For what felt like an eternity, their gazes locked.

Natalie's every instinct told her Wyatt had a rebuttal to her impromptu speech, but for whatever reason, he wasn't prepared to use it.

"That's the way you feel," he said with a resigned nod, "can't say as I blame you."

Why didn't he fight for her—for himself?

When she'd shown up at his house, he'd seemed genuinely excited to see her. The kind of excitement that might one day lead to more. Now, he didn't seem to care. About her. The baby. Anything.

That fact hurt more than he'd ever know.

"HERE YOU GO." AFTER the dance, Wyatt stopped his truck in front of Natalie's little white house.

He put the truck in Park, killed the engine, then climbed out to open her door.

"I can manage," she argued in typical Natalie style.

"I'm sure you can, but you asked me to be your escort for the night and until I've seen you safely inside, I'm responsible for you."

"That's a ridiculously antiquated notion." Sticking her key in the lock, she turned the dead bolt on her door.

"Like your assumption every man on the planet will abandon you the same as Craig?" Wyatt hadn't wanted to cause a scene at the school, but she'd seriously pushed his buttons.

Natalie shoved him aside to push her way into the house.

He followed.

"Did I invite you in?" she asked, turning on a lamp before tossing her purse on the entry hall table.

"Sorry," he said, "but this is one time you don't get a vote."

"In *my* house, I always get a vote."

They stood toe to toe, each breathing hard. "What I have to say might take a while, so if you don't mind, have a seat before your feet explode."

"Right now," she snapped, "I'm more concerned with my bladder."

Raking his fingers through his hair, he said, "Take

a brief bathroom intermission and then get yourself back in here on the sofa."

She raised her chin. "I'd be more comfortable in bed."

Roaring in frustration, he said, "Woman, I don't give a damn if you sit on a lawn chair in the garage. Do what you have to do in the bathroom and then we're going to talk."

While waiting, he made himself at home in her room, turning on bedside lamps and studying her few framed pictures. One with her and Josie both looking considerably younger, hamming it up at Weed Gulch's only mini golf course. Another more recent with her parents. Then there were a trio of her with Craig. At the Tulsa Zoo and a beach and skiing. The two had been together for years. Wyatt would have bet major coin on Craig having been in the relationship with Natalie for the long haul.

"Here I am," Natalie finally said, out of the bathroom and her fancy dress. She now wore gray Weed Gulch Varsity Football sweats. Her former tower of hair leaned to the right, and with her makeup removed, her skin was pale. Passing Wyatt, she tossed back her comforter and top sheet and crawled into bed. Once she'd pulled the covers over herself, then plumped the down pillows behind her head, she closed her eyes and sighed. "This is where I've wanted to be for the past four hours."

"You should've said something. I'd have brought you home."

"I couldn't shirk my duty."

He sat on the bed next to her. "No one would've held it against you."

"Whatever." Arms tightly folded across her chest,

she said, "Please get on with what you need to say. I'm ready for bed."

"The short version is that I'm pretty sure I've fallen for you in a way I never thought I would."

"Pretty sure?" she all but shrieked. "This is the kind of thing I'm talking about, Wyatt. News flash—I'm going to be a mother. The last thing I need is a week-ends-only boyfriend."

"What if I told you I want more?"

"I wouldn't believe you." Hands over her face, she shook her head. "And regardless, I'll never settle for anything less than marriage."

"Done." Pulse racing to a degree that made Wyatt not entirely certain he wasn't having a heart attack, he licked suddenly dry lips. *Don't do this,* his conscience urged. *You don't love her. You don't even know what love is. Just because you two had a semi-successful run at playing house doesn't mean you should try it again. Especially not in an official capacity.* Overriding all voices of reason, Wyatt said, "Marry me. Give me the chance to be a dad to your son. You've seen me with Dallas and Josie's girls. You know I'll make a great father."

"Are you even listening to the insanity coming out of your mouth? You don't want to marry me. I'm carrying another man's child. Worse yet, say I agree to your proposal? What then? Because if you marry me in front of God and our families only to one day leave…"

Leaning forward, Wyatt kissed her with every shred of emotion he had in him. "Nat, you're under my skin. The whole time I was in Alaska, all I thought about was getting home. Only without you in it, my house feels empty. I need you and your son to make me whole."

"This is crazy," she said with a firm shake of her head. "You're crazy."

"And?" After kissing her again and again, he drew back and said, "Natalie Grace Lewis, will you marry me?"

Chapter Fourteen

"Yes," Natalie managed to choke out through messy tears. "I will marry you." Logic told her this was madness. Her heart said Wyatt's sincerity to do right by her and her son was true. If it seemed too easy, that's probably because it was right. For all of her insisting she wanted to be a single mom, a shared life with Wyatt sounded much more fun.

"Yes?" He wore an adorable half smile, looking part exhilarated, part terrified.

"Want me to change my mind?"

Laughing, he said, "Nah. But before we let anyone else in on our news, how about stealing the rest of tonight for just us?"

"If that means what I think it does, I suddenly feel energized."

"Great," he said with a sexy growl, "because I feel horny for my future wife."

AFTER A FULL NIGHT SPENT doing just about everything but sleeping, Natalie should've been exhausted. Instead, she sat snuggled against Wyatt in his truck, excited for Georgina's Sunday brunch. Typically, she just looked forward to the caramel nut rolls and thick-sliced hickory bacon, but she had a feeling today's announcement would be tastier than anything she might eat.

"What're you thinking about?" Natalie asked Wyatt as he turned onto the main house's drive. Tracing his furrowed eyebrows, she fought a twinge of unease. Getting married was a big step. It was understandable Wyatt would have the occasional serious moment.

"Nothing you need worry about."

"That kind of evasive answer makes me worry more." As he parked the truck and turned off the engine, she slid to the far side of the leather bench seat. Clutching her purse, her fingertips felt icy. "If you're having second thoughts, please tell me now. Don't put me through the indignity of celebrating with my closest friends and then calling it off."

Snagging her by her waist, he slid her against him, pressing an affectionate kiss to her forehead. "If every time my mind wanders you're going to assume the worst, we might have a problem."

"You're not having second thoughts?"

"Get it through your thick, beautiful head. I like you—a lot."

After a sharp exhale, she fought tears.

With the pad of his thumb, Wyatt brushed them from her cheeks. "There's no crying at our engagement announcement."

Nodding, crying more, she said, "Sorry. I feel impossibly full—like everything I've ever wanted is coming true. But if I so much as blink, it could vanish as easily as it appeared."

"Good grief." He kissed her and then kissed her more. "Let's hurry up and get this news out in the open. The sooner Mom starts planning our wedding, the sooner we can actually get hitched."

"Think we can do it before the baby comes?"

Blasting her with his slow, sexy grin, he said, "Not if we don't get out of this truck."

"PLEASE DON'T TELL ME your trip to Ethiopia is back on," Georgina said prior to Wyatt and Natalie's announcement. "Because if that's what you made me stop eating to hear, I'll be mighty grumpy."

"Relax," Natalie urged Wyatt's mom. "It's nothing like that."

Josie turned to Natalie. "You're in on his big secret?"

Natalie's sweet smile lit the room. "You might say that."

"Out with it," Dallas said in a lighthearted tone, "before my food gets cold."

"Yeah," Bonnie said. "Mine, too."

Reaching across the table for Natalie's hands, Wyatt stood. "Last night, I asked Natalie to marry me and she accepted."

Georgina shrieked, then clapped. "I knew you two had funny business going on."

"How could you keep this from me?" Josie demanded, swatting her friend with her cloth napkin.

Laughing and ducking, Natalie said, "He only asked last night. Trust me, you all are the first to know."

"We knew a *looong* time ago," Betsy said.

"Yeah." Bonnie held three strips of bacon to her mouth. "We knew all the way back when Uncle Wyatt put his hands on Miss Natalie's butt."

"Butt!" Mabel shouted. "Butt, butt, butt!"

OVER SUNDAY SUPPER, UPON digesting Natalie's exciting news, Opal burst into tears. "You have no idea how relieved this makes me. I thought Ian would be a good match for you, but you probably had Wyatt on your mind all along."

"Hold up, Mother. Don't go getting too excited just yet," Bud said. "No offense, but Wyatt, around these parts, you've got a bit of a wild reputation. Why all of a sudden have you now decided to settle down?"

Frowning, her mother said, "Natalie, your father does have a point."

"Wow." Opal's sweet-potato casserole soured on Natalie's tongue. "You all are some pieces of work. First, you're upset with me for being pregnant without a husband. Now, you're unhappy because I didn't choose the right one?"

"That's not at all what your father's saying." Patting her napkin to the corners of her mouth, Opal said, "You have to admit, Wyatt Buckhorn seems an unlikely choice. He's over thirty and never been in a committed relationship. He goes off for weeks and months at a time, traveling for that oil job of his, and my gut tells me it's not him you love, but the Buckhorn fast and fancy lifestyle. Ever since your friend Josie married into them, you've been—"

"Mrs. Lewis," Wyatt said, "I've sat through nearly this entire meal biting my tongue. You can insult me all you want, but once you bring my family into it, you and I have a problem. All you need to know is that your daughter means the world to me. And I'm excited to be a father for her son."

Bud helped himself to seconds of ham. "That's all I need to hear. Mother, that satisfy you?"

"Yes and no," Opal said, "part of me still wonders why Wyatt hasn't married—or even been with the same woman for any length of time? Is there something about him we don't know? For that matter, as much as I've been praying for our girl to find a husband, hasn't this happened awfully fast? Have either of you thought this through?"

"Thank you for the food," Natalie somehow said past a throat so tight with tears that finding air had become a challenge. "I'll send you a wedding invitation. Please don't feel obligated to come."

Natalie waited until Wyatt had driven to the end of her parents' block before she broke down. "Wh-why are they crazy?" she wailed. "Why can't they be happy for me?"

"That's it." Wyatt pulled to the curb, placing the truck in Park. Hugging her, he said, "Let it out."

"Th-this was supposed to have been a happy night. I thought my parents w-would be thrilled."

"Deep down," he said with a half chuckle, "I'm sure they are."

"H-how could they be so cruel? I—I adore your family. Th-they've all been wonderful to me. D-Dallas is a little scary, but I'd much r-rather be locked with him in a closet than my p-parents."

"Hey, whoa," he protested, a smile lighting his eyes, "kindly keep your sexy self away from closets and my brothers."

"Y-you know what I mean."

"Yes, I do," he said, "but, sweetie, you have to admit, they raised a few valid points."

"I appreciate you trying to make peace, but don't for a second search their motives for justification when there's none."

THROUGHOUT THE TWO WEEKS leading up to his wedding, Wyatt couldn't keep Opal's tirade from his mind.

What he'd repeatedly tried reminding Natalie was that her mother had been right. There was a reason he'd remained single for so long. Commitment scared the hell out of him. Worse, was Natalie sure she wanted to marry a man who would never give her the big fairy-tale family she craved? But each time he tried to have a serious conversation, Natalie shut him down.

The women of his family had transformed into wedding-planning whirlwinds. Natalie constantly reminded him how little time they had not just until their big day, but until their son was born.

Their son.

Most men Wyatt knew would have issues raising another man's child. He viewed the opportunity as a blessing. He ignored the question of what happened a year or two down the line when Natalie wanted more children he couldn't provide.

On this day, he sat patiently in his mother's dining room, listening to a panel of caterers vie for what would no doubt be a huge job. He and Natalie had both worked all day. Wyatt worried about her overdoing it, but she'd assured him that Georgina, his sister and sisters-in-law had done the majority of planning.

"Wyatt?" Natalie elbowed his ribs. "If you don't taste each dish, how are you going to vote?"

"Sweetheart, how about you surprise me and I promise to love everything you pick."

Natalie's death-ray stare told Wyatt he'd said the wrong thing.

"Or," he smiled, "I could pay closer attention to these delicious offerings and cast a well-educated vote."

By the time the caterers left, it was already dark and Natalie had stopped trying to hide her yawns. "What's wrong with me?" she complained. "My back aches and I'm exhausted."

"You don't think you're going into labor, do you?"

She shook her head. "I'm not due for another two weeks, and all of my books say first babies are usually late."

"Think we should call Doc Haven? Just to be safe?"

Wrinkling her nose, Natalie said, "I don't want to interrupt this special night with a false alarm."

She thanked his mom and the other three ladies present, and then made the same rounds with all of the kids and babies. Even Prissy had come over for the food tasting.

Kitty sat on the grand piano, showing his disdain.

"Come on," Wyatt said when it looked as if the twins might talk Natalie into staying for a movie. "Let's get you home and in bed. Otherwise, you're going to sleep through work in the morning."

"All right," she complained, holding out her arms when he helped her into her warm wool coat. "I get the hint that you're going to be the kind of husband who works me till my fingers bleed."

Ignoring her, as well as every other woman's jab, he ushered his bride-to-be to the truck and hefted her onto the passenger seat.

Wyatt hoped to bring up his concerns on the ride home, but Natalie fell asleep. Her soft snores made him smile. That told him he'd be a fool not to want to marry a woman this adorable.

At Natalie's house, it took a while to wake her.

"Want me to carry you?"

"No. I'm not an invalid. Just—" As she toddled toward the house, her water broke, trailing in a steaming path up the sidewalk. "Oh, no."

"Oh, yes." They'd been so focused on having the wedding before the baby that the poor kid had taken a temporary backseat. "Let's not panic. We haven't even packed you a suitcase, and that baby book says that's one of the most important things about going into labor."

"Right now, I think getting to the hospital might be a higher priority."

"Okay, um—" Wyatt's head started to spin. He was going to be a father. But how could he adequately do that when he couldn't even get the kid's mom to the hospital with the right gear? "You need candles and that new age ocean and whale song music."

In the house, heading toward the bathroom, she said, "I'd rather listen to Taking Back Sunday or Aerosmith."

"No," he argued, raiding her closet and dresser for baby-delivery-appropriate clothes. "The book was quite clear on having soothing music in the birthing room."

In the bedroom, she asked, "What happened to *my* Wyatt? I'm pretty sure you're not him."

"I'm being responsible. Is your camera battery charged and do you have plenty of memory cards?"

"I know this is a big deal," she started rummaging through her dresser drawers, "but last I checked, my card holds almost a thousand pictures. I think we're fine with only one."

"Just in case, we'll stop off at a Walmart on the way into Tulsa."

She'd gathered a change of clothes and returned to the bathroom.

"What are you doing?" He followed. "This is an emergency. We have to go."

"News flash, baby expert! I peed myself with amniotic fluid. I'm taking a shower before going anywhere."

"Should I get in with you? Make sure you're all right?"

"You're crazy," she said while shimmying out of her tights. "Not only am I reconsidering marrying you, but I might have you banned from the delivery room."

"Really?" His heart sank.

On her tiptoes, she kissed him. "Not really. But, angel, you've got to relax. Everything's going to be fine."

EIGHTEEN HOURS LATER, Natalie was hot and cold and so far from fine she seriously regretted blowing off Lamaze. Agony didn't begin describing the reality of childbirth. All those idyllic magazine shots of blissful moms in the delivery room? Lies!

"Wyatt?"

"Right here, sweetheart." He'd been seated in a rocker at the head of her bed, but now stood. "What do you need?"

"Ask when I can have an epidural."

"Yes, ma'am." He kissed her forehead. "Be right back."

"Poor thing," Josie crooned, holding a cold cloth to Natalie's forehead. "It may not seem like it now, but when you finally hold your baby in your arms, this will all be worth it."

"If I survive."

"You'll be fine," her best friend assured.

Wyatt returned with a nurse.

"I heard you could use a little relief?"

Wincing through her latest contraction, Natalie managed a nod.

"I've put out a call for the anesthesiologist, but it could take anywhere from ten minutes to an hour for him to get here."

Hovering at the foot of the bed, Wyatt said, "If we had that ocean relaxation CD the book talked about, it might help."

Was it wrong that Natalie wanted to leap from the bed and strangle the man she was about to marry? "For the last time, I don't want to hear whales or seagulls or anything other than my ob-gyn announcing my baby's a healthy boy."

"What if you accidentally have a girl?" the nurse asked.

"Does that happen?" Natalie raised her brows. "The ultrasound people flub their predictions?"

"Not often, but I have seen it. Usually it turns out that little girls are actually boys."

The nurse finished recording Natalie's vitals before leaving the room.

Natalie finally got her epidural, which helped, but didn't completely numb the pain. What did bring comfort was Wyatt constantly by her side. He fed her ice chips and rubbed her neck and was the only one not cracking jokes about her needing three pairs of socks on her freezing feet.

Hour after hour passed.

Natalie's parents stopped by, but when Opal made a move to make herself comfortable in the delivery room, Wyatt ushered her and Bud out to the waiting room where they could sit surrounded by Buckhorns.

Finally, the time came to push.

Wyatt's voice became a tranquil pool in the midst of an awful storm. When she screamed, no matter how hard she squeezed his hand, he never let go. And when the baby finally crowned, and she felt as if she were being torn apart, he held on still, urging her forward with dear words of encouragement.

"That's it," Wyatt urged, "push, angel, push. You can do it. This baby's going to make our family whole."

"You're almost done," her doctor said. "Just a little more."

Natalie screamed and bore down. She had never worked so hard for anything. And then the pain was gone.

"Congratulations, mama," her nurse said. "You have a handsome baby boy. Know what you want to name him?"

Laughing, crying, trembling as the nurse set the baby to Natalie's chest, she shook her head. "Look, Wyatt, at how perfect he is."

"He's a full-on miracle." Wyatt had teared up, as well.

"His fingers are so tiny." Natalie wondered at her little man. Never had she fallen for a guy so fast. "I love you."

"I can already tell I love him, too." What Wyatt wasn't certain of in that moment was had he asked Natalie to marry him out of genuine emotion, or the desire to be a father to her baby? Because at the moment, he was so overcome by what he'd just witnessed, he couldn't be sure.

Chapter Fifteen

One week into parenthood, Wyatt's stomach had settled into a permanent knot.

He didn't think it was possible, but Natalie's son, Micah, felt like his own. Life had never been more perfect, yet at the same time more of a lie.

With the wedding being held a week from Saturday, Wyatt felt dishonorable. As if in even proposing to Natalie, he'd hitched a ride on her happy train. Had he truly fallen for her, or was he with her only for her child? If that was the case, how could he do that to Natalie, caring for her as he did?

While Natalie slept, Wyatt rocked Micah, memorizing every inch of his face. The way his eyelashes swept his cheeks and how even though he was sleeping, his lips still suckled. His skin was impossibly soft and blemish-free. Just like his conscience.

Wyatt couldn't ever remember not harboring guilt over one thing or another. As a kid, he'd constantly been in trouble. As a teen, he hadn't been much better. For a while he'd tried unsuccessfully to be a responsible adult, but upon asking Natalie to marry him, all that had changed.

"You two look handsome together."

Wyatt glanced up to see Natalie in her sleep-rumpled glory. "Pretty sure this beast's magnetism is rubbing off on me."

Holding out her arms, she smiled, "Give me our little angel."

Wyatt handed Natalie the baby before joining her on the bed.

"Funny how everything turned out," she said. "After all the time we spent with Esther, I actually feel somewhat competent with Micah—except for breast-feeding. It's trickier than it looks."

"I wouldn't know," he said with a straight face. "Though last time I tried, the process seemed fairly straightforward."

"If I didn't need both hands for holding our baby, you'd be in serious trouble, Mr. Buckhorn."

"Soon-to-be Mrs. Buckhorn, bring it on. But when you're done pummeling me, I want to talk."

"About what?" Taking pink baby lotion from the nightstand, she squirted a dab into her palm, then rubbed it onto the baby's hands and forearms.

Wyatt took a fortifying breath, searching for the right words. "I wish I had— No, I wanted to—"

Natalie's cell rang. "Hold that thought. It's probably your mom. She has questions about the flowers."

The caller did turn out to be Georgina, and after an initial discussion on the merits of tulips versus daffodils, the conversation turned to cake—three or five tier. Band versus DJ or both. And on and on and on.

Wyatt couldn't give a flip about having a lavish wedding, but it seemed important to Natalie and his mom.

Sensing his bride was only getting warmed up on the issue of linen colors, Wyatt kidnapped Micah and took him to the living room for male bonding over OU basketball.

Fate would ultimately decide when the time was right for Wyatt to ask Natalie if she thought they were rushing things. More important, if she thought what they shared was genuine, last-a-lifetime love. Or was it just excitement over the baby? Until then, he wouldn't waste a second with the precious child.

AT THE REHEARSAL DINNER, Wyatt slipped his arm around Natalie's shoulders just as Dallas hit the tines of his fork to his champagne flute.

"If I could have everyone's attention." Dallas raised his glass. "Can't believe the day has finally come, but tomorrow, the last of the Buckhorn clan is getting married. Even better, Wyatt's bride happens to be my wife's best friend, Natalie. As if that weren't enough to make this an extra-special occasion, Natalie is also bringing her son, Micah, to the family."

Georgina currently had hold of the baby and showed no signs of letting go.

"When my brother was a little kid," Dallas continued, "one of his favorite things to do was rein Ralph the donkey to an old wagon. He'd drive that poor donkey all over hell and creation, not playing cowboys and Indians, but wagon train. He'd pretend the dogs were his kids, and his wife, well, she was a scarecrow he'd found in a corner of the barn."

"Hey," Wyatt said in his defense above the laughter, "she was a seriously hot scarecrow."

"Sure, bro. Anyway, making a long story short, I couldn't be happier my brother Wyatt has a beautiful family worthy of leading down the Oregon Trail. And while I'm assuming the happy couple won't be setting out for the West Coast anytime soon, they are embarking on what I hope will be a fulfilling lifelong journey for them both."

"Hear, hear!" Georgina called out. "To the bride and groom! May your marriage trail be pothole-free and filled with the bounty of love."

"Not sure what that last part meant," Wyatt whispered to Natalie, "but I'm all for the toasting." While their friends and family clinked glasses, he and Natalie shared a champagne-flavored kiss.

"Wagon train is the best game ever, isn't it? Did the guys on your football team know what you did after practice?"

"Ha-ha," he complained. "I was ten."

"I think it's hot." Pressing against him, she said in a sex-kitten purr, "Big, strong you protecting me and itty bitty Micah from mountain lions and bears. We could cuddle up at night in front of the campfire, feeding each other bites of beef jerky."

"Don't forget smoked salmon." He stole a kiss. "I love that stuff."

"Absolutely. We'll add to my part of the wedding vows that I'll always keep a big supply of salmon on hand for my man."

Though they were only playing around, Wyatt wished he could make her the same kind of blanket promise. Loving, protecting and cherishing Micah was the easy job. It was everything else that had him worried.

"What's wrong?" she asked, tracing his frown lines. "You look like you just lost your best friend."

I'm afraid I will.

He needed to come clean about his fears, but obviously the middle of their rehearsal dinner wasn't the right time. But if not now, when? The clock was ticking. If he didn't tell her before the wedding, and for whatever reason, things between them didn't work out, he wouldn't blame her if she never talked to him again.

"I'm good," he said. "Overwhelmed. I've gotta confess this is a place I never expected to be." He gestured to the opulence around them: his mother's fairy-tale wedding theme, complete with a temporary castle for them to be wed in; the hundreds, maybe even thousands of spring flowers—lilacs and daffodils and tulips. All of his siblings' weddings had been grand, but since his was the last, his mother had explained, she'd wanted it to rival royalty. Because that's what the Buckhorns were. Oklahoma royalty.

"Me, neither," Natalie admitted. "But how lucky are we? I don't mean about the fancy wedding—although it is going to be nothing short of amazing—but for us to have sort of discovered each other after all these years. I can't stop pinching myself. I remember once telling you I'd settle for nothing less than my very own Prince Charming, and here you are."

Eyes shining with unshed tears, she stood on her tiptoes to kiss him.

Lord, he didn't want to hurt this woman. But then if he really meant that, he'd have never proposed. The truth was, no matter how badly he wanted her dream for their happily-ever-after to come true, as long as she was marrying him, he feared her happy ending was unlikely.

"I'VE NEVER SEEN A MORE beautiful bride," Josie gushed to Natalie. Because of its easy access to the faux-stone castle Georgina had constructed—complete with a moat—the ranch's guest cabin was being used for the bridal suite.

"I agree," Cami said. "You're glowing."

Considering the outrageous opulence of her ivory satin dress, it would be impossible for any woman not to glow. The skirt was full like a storybook princess's and the veil made of ivory lace so fine she was afraid heavy breathing might cause a tear. A styling team had been brought in from Tulsa to do the wedding party's makeup and hair. Natalie's upswept 'do featured crystals and pearls.

Josie, Daisy, Cami and Wren served as bridesmaids. Their dresses were a parade of satin ball gowns in celebratory shades of spring. Their hair had been swept high with fresh flowers matching their dresses' colors.

Georgina had been in and out, but mostly out. As the chief wedding planner, her proverbial plate wasn't just full, but heaped and threatening to topple.

"In case I haven't told you enough," Josie said, "I'm insanely happy for you. Wyatt is such a good man. You two are going to have an amazing life."

"Are you living in his house or yours?" Wren asked Natalie.

The bride laughed. "If you'd seen the size of mine, you'd know it's not even a question."

Daisy said, "Wyatt's place is an architectural wonder."

Wren asked Daisy, "How long until your house is finished?"

Making a strangling gesture, Daisy said, "Considering we've just fired our fourth stonemason, we're hoping to be in by May. I never knew there could be so many little things to go wrong."

"This is off topic," Natalie said, "but before the day gets away from me, I want you all to know how excited

I am to become an official Buckhorn. I've been crashing your family parties forever, so it'll be nice from now on to have a standing invitation."

"Aw," Daisy said. "Group hug."

Getting four full skirts out of the way enough to embrace was no easy feat, but Natalie's throat swelled in gratitude that they did.

A knock sounded on the cabin door.

"Let me get it," Josie said. "I don't want any of the groomsmen barging their way in."

"Bud, Opal," Josie said, her tone less than thrilled. Natalie's stomach sank. She loved her parents, but lately, no matter what she did, they didn't seem to be on her side. They were, however, enamored with their grandson, who was currently sacked out in his wicker bassinet.

"Honey," Natalie's mother said, "you look stunning. Your father and I couldn't be happier for you."

"Really?" Because the last time they'd talked, her mother had still been dubious as to the degree of Wyatt's commitment.

Bud nodded. "I'm sorry for our initial reaction to your engagement. After seeing how great Wyatt is with Micah, we understand what you see in him. He's not the same man Weed Gulch labeled the town's only professional bachelor."

"Thanks, Dad." Fighting back tears so as not to ruin her makeup, she gave him and her mother a hug.

After checking on their grandson, Natalie's parents left.

Their blessing had been the whipped cream and cherry on top of her already perfect day.

When there was another knock, Natalie assumed her

parents had forgotten something. Maybe her borrowed item or something blue?

Josie called that she'd get it, but Natalie beat her to it.

She tossed open the door, expecting to be handed her mother's prized pearl bracelet. Her expectations were right—along with a bonus teary hug.

Natalie wanted to be one hundred percent immersed in her dewy bridal role, but she couldn't get Wyatt's haunted look from the night before to leave her brain. What had been troubling him? Would she ever know?

STANDING AT THE ALTAR, spring sun warm on his face, Wyatt wanted to feel complete. As if his every dream were on the verge of coming true.

Cami walked down the aisle, followed by Wyatt's sister and two sisters-in-law.

Alongside him stood Dallas, Cash, Luke and Kolt.

The castle his mother had designed was insane—but in a good way. The massive rectangular space had been constructed of wood and then covered in faux stone. A drawbridge led guests and the wedding party to a two-story great hall complete with a retractable roof—since any time of year Oklahoma weather could be iffy. The altar end featured a three-level stage on which towered antique candelabras and enough blooms to make the entire space smell of spring. Stained-glass windows were each fronted by ornamental peach trees in bloom.

Wyatt had to hand it to his mother. He didn't have a clue where she came up with her outlandish party ideas, but he was glad this one had been used on him. The moat she'd had dug to surround the castle even had fountains. Because who didn't want to hear tinkling water mingling with their string octet?

As grand as the wedding's backdrop, nothing compared to the wonder of Natalie walking down the aisle, accompanied by her father and son. Natalie had her hands full with an enormous draping bouquet. Bud pushed a decorated baby carriage, and though Natalie's dad typically wore a scowl, on this day he smiled.

Her whole walk, Wyatt tried holding Natalie's gaze, but in the end, he couldn't. Her baby held him in a spell. How long had he dreamt of having his own child?

Wyatt would be the best imaginable father, but this ceremony, this moment, wasn't about Micah, but the little guy's mother. Didn't Natalie deserve the same degree of love and adoration? What was wrong with him that he felt dubious as to whether he had it in him to give?

Once Wyatt's bride reached him, and her father had officially given her and Micah away, Wyatt assumed he'd feel better. More at peace. Instead, the more he took in her emotion-filled expression, the more he knew he couldn't sustain this lie. How was he ever going to know if he loved Natalie enough to marry her? He felt as if she was his best friend, but shouldn't there be something more?

The singsong rhythm of their vows brought on a headache. And then heartache when it struck him what he had to do.

"Natalie Grace Lewis," their family pastor said while his mother softly cried in the front row, "will you take Wyatt William Buckhorn to be your lawfully wedded husband? To have and to hold? For richer or poorer? For the rest of your lifelong days?"

Instead of going ahead and answering so Wyatt

could get on with what would surely break her heart, as if she had a bee in her ear, Natalie shook her head. "I'm sorry. Really, *really* sorry, but Wyatt, I can't marry you."

Just like that, she snatched her baby from his festooned carriage and ran off down the aisle.

"Nat," Wyatt called, "wait!" He'd been on the verge of backing out on her, but now that she'd done it first, he wasn't so sure about anything anymore—especially when it came to the matter of not loving her. For if he truly didn't, why did it hurt so bad seeing her go?

Chasing after her, calling her name, he finally caught up in the guest cabin, only to find her struggling to escape her gown.

"Nat," he managed, out of breath, bracing his hands on his knees, "sweetie, we need to talk."

"Don't you *sweetie* me," she snapped. "You've been acting strange for days, ever since the wedding planning went into high gear. You've pouted and scowled and had me wondering if you were sick or scared or hiding a horrible secret." Conking her forehead with the heel of her hand, she said, "Don't know how I could've been such a fool not to have recognized this before, but it was never me you loved—just Micah. Walking down the aisle, I couldn't wait for you to see me in this gorgeous dress. But when I looked at you, hoping to see love—or at least deep affection—you never once took your eyes off my son."

Mind reeling, Wyatt wasn't sure what to do. How had this day gone so horribly wrong? She was right, but he all of a sudden didn't want her to be.

"You and me—*us,*" she said in a barely audible tone, "it was all a lie, wasn't it? You wanted a son, and by sheer coincidence, I just happened to be having one."

"You're talking crazy," he managed. "I mean, yeah, I might've felt like that a little while ago, but in the split second you left me, I knew I'd be lost without you."

"Save it." She put her fingers over his lips. "This is just like Craig all over again except in reverse. He dumped me because of our child, and you only want me for my child."

"Would you listen?" he implored. "I admit, looking back on it, I may not have consciously entered into this with the best of intentions. But I was a fool. Hell, trust the feelings we've had simmering for each other since grade school."

"No." She was unable to see him through her tears. Heavy mascara stung her eyes. How many times had she told herself Wyatt was all wrong for her? Why, *why* had she thought for one moment her dreams of having a perfect family might actually come true? "That wasn't love, but lust. I deserve more."

"I know, angel, which is why—" He'd grasped her forearms, but she pushed him away.

"Where's my purse? I—I have to get out of here. Get away."

"Let me get this straight—you're escaping from me?"

"If that's what you want to call it. You do happen to be the expert on running away."

"But I didn't run. Remember?" Raising his chin, he said, "I never ran during the time we watched the girls and I'm not the one who ran out of our wedding. Now, I know, beyond all reasonable doubt the churning in my stomach over the past few days wasn't fear of being committed to you and Micah, but fear of not having that official level of commitment. I love you. I love our

Chapter Sixteen

"Shhh…" Three weeks later, Natalie unfastened Micah's safety harness, lifting him into her arms. "It's okay, pumpkin. Just a few more minutes and we'll get you fed and settled down."

With the baby wailing all the way, Natalie rushed up the path to the cabin/tent Wyatt reportedly called home. The Rift Valley Safari Lodge was where he and his crew had set up their base camp in Ethiopia's Rift Valley. From what she'd seen on TV, she'd have expected the place to be mercilessly hot and void of vegetation, but the "Roof of Africa" had turned out to be a beautiful surprise. Though there was plenty of hard-packed red dirt, there were also an abundance of trees and a nearby river.

Pulse racing, she asked herself what was the worst that could happen? Wyatt rejecting her? No biggie, considering she'd first rejected him. His expression while she'd walked down the aisle had led her to bolt. Who was to say whether he'd intended to or not? Maybe if she'd stuck around, they might already be married and living in his pretty forest house. Instead, she'd been forced to beg Georgina and Dallas to use some of their considerable pull to obtain visas for both her and Micah.

Georgina and Natalie's parents both felt Micah shouldn't go, but Doc Haven had given her baby the required immunizations and she'd made sure to keep him covered to protect him from mosquitoes. She needed Micah to remind Wyatt that the two of them were a package deal.

If only she'd paused a moment before her outburst, she'd have remembered how deep Wyatt's love of children ran. Her accusations had been both ludicrous and insulting. Her only hope of regaining the dream she'd all but thrown away was to go to her man. If he'd been afraid of love, so what? So had she. Together, they had a lifetime to work through it.

Trying the door and finding it unlocked, she let herself in. "Wyatt?"

He didn't answer, but over Micah's cries, she heard the shower.

Spying a wooden rocker much like the one in her cabin, she sat and then offered her breast to her ravenous son.

When the noise from the shower spray stopped, her pulse raced. Would Wyatt be happy to see her and Micah? Sad? Angry?

"Nat?"

She looked up to see him sporting a full beard and wild hair in need of a trim. His skin was deeply tanned. Never, in all the years she'd known him, had he looked so good.

"Hope you don't mind the intrusion." She cast him a faint smile. "Micah told me he missed his dad."

Wearing a towel, Wyatt knelt on the tile floor, stroking Micah's cheek. "He's even more handsome than I remembered."

Still feasting, Micah never took his gaze from his father. No matter what, Natalie would always think of Wyatt in that way.

"I owe you an apology," she said. "I was so afraid of you leaving me, I left you first."

"Truthfully, I did think of walking out on our wedding. I didn't trust that it was realistic for me to love two people so deeply at once."

Lower lip trembling, she bit it to keep from crying. "That was such a hectic time. We needed more space to be with each other, rather than with florists and bakers and caterers."

"I know."

She cupped her hand to his dear cheek. "I love you. Micah loves you. *Please* forgive me. Marry me. Here. Back in Weed Gulch. As long as we're all together, the details don't matter."

Eyes pooling, he said, "It should be criminal for a man to feel this full." Grazing the top of Micah's head with the underside of his chin, he added, "And if it's all the same to you, I'd prefer to skip my mother's hoopla in favor of a more intimate ceremony. I want to show you a great waterfall I spotted the day I first arrived."

Emotions bubbled over, leaving Natalie in a hyper-aware state in which she wasn't sure whether to laugh or cry. She'd come perilously close to losing the only man she'd ever truly loved. The thought was terrifying, but in the same sense, motivational to once and for all get the wedding vows done.

THE NEXT MORNING, SURROUNDED by his few work buddies and the lodge owners, Wyatt stood in front of a thundering waterfall. Rainbows hung in the mist.

This time, when his bride came to him, holding Micah in her arms, he only had eyes for her. Did a part of him wish his family was there? Sure. But not enough to have postponed his destiny for one second more. In Natalie, he'd finally found a friend, lover and wife. How long had he wasted worrying about his condition when in the end, it hadn't mattered? All that did was love.

* * * * *

HEART & HOME

Heartwarming romances where love can
happen right when you least expect it.

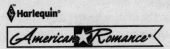

COMING NEXT MONTH
AVAILABLE JANUARY 10, 2012

#1385 HIS VALENTINE TRIPLETS
Callahan Cowboys
Tina Leonard

#1386 THE COWBOY'S SECRET SON
The Teagues of Texas
Trish Milburn

#1387 THE SEAL'S PROMISE
Undercover Heroes
Rebecca Winters

#1388 CLAIMED BY A COWBOY
Hill Country Heroes
Tanya Michaels

REQUEST YOUR FREE BOOKS!
2 FREE NOVELS PLUS 2 FREE GIFTS!

LOVE, HOME & HAPPINESS

YES! Please send me 2 FREE Harlequin® American Romance® novels and my 2 FREE gifts (gifts are worth about $10). After receiving them, if I don't wish to receive any more books, I can return the shipping statement marked "cancel." If I don't cancel, I will receive 4 brand-new novels every month and be billed just $4.49 per book in the U.S. or $5.24 per book in Canada. That's a saving of at least 14% off the cover price! It's quite a bargain! Shipping and handling is just 50¢ per book in the U.S. and 75¢ per book in Canada.* I understand that accepting the 2 free books and gifts places me under no obligation to buy anything. I can always return a shipment and cancel at any time. Even if I never buy another book, the two free books and gifts are mine to keep forever.

154/354 HDN FEP2

Name	(PLEASE PRINT)	
Address		Apt. #
City	State/Prov.	Zip/Postal Code

Signature (if under 18, a parent or guardian must sign)

Mail to the Reader Service:
IN U.S.A.: P.O. Box 1867, Buffalo, NY 14240-1867
IN CANADA: P.O. Box 609, Fort Erie, Ontario L2A 5X3

Not valid for current subscribers to Harlequin American Romance books.

Want to try two free books from another line?
Call 1-800-873-8635 or visit www.ReaderService.com.

* Terms and prices subject to change without notice. Prices do not include applicable taxes. Sales tax applicable in N.Y. Canadian residents will be charged applicable taxes. Offer not valid in Quebec. This offer is limited to one order per household. All orders subject to credit approval. Credit or debit balances in a customer's account(s) may be offset by any other outstanding balance owed by or to the customer. Please allow 4 to 6 weeks for delivery. Offer available while quantities last.

Your Privacy—The Reader Service is committed to protecting your privacy. Our Privacy Policy is available online at www.ReaderService.com or upon request from the Reader Service.

We make a portion of our mailing list available to reputable third parties that offer products we believe may interest you. If you prefer that we not exchange your name with third parties, or if you wish to clarify or modify your communication preferences, please visit us at www.ReaderService.com/consumerschoice or write to us at Reader Service Preference Service, P.O. Box 9062, Buffalo, NY 14269. Include your complete name and address.

HARI1B

SPECIAL EDITION

Life, Love and Family

Karen Templeton

introduces

The FORTUNES *of* TEXAS: Whirlwind Romance

When a tornado destroys Red Rock, Texas,
Christina Hastings finds herself trapped in the
rubble with telecommunications heir
Scott Fortune. He's handsome, smart and
everything Christina has learned to guard herself
against. As they await rescue, an unlikely attraction
forms between the two and Scott soon finds
himself wanting to know about this mysterious
beauty. But can he catch Christina before she runs
away from her true feelings?

FORTUNE'S CINDERELLA

Available December 27th wherever books are sold!

*Brittany Grayson survived a horrible ordeal at the hands of a serial killer known as The Professional...
who's after her now?*

Harlequin® Romantic Suspense presents a new installment in Carla Cassidy's reader-favorite miniseries,
LAWMEN OF BLACK ROCK.

Enjoy a sneak peek of
TOOL BELT DEFENDER.

*Available January 2012
from Harlequin® Romantic Suspense.*

"**B**rittany?" His voice was deep and pleasant and made her realize she'd been staring at him openmouthed through the screen door.

"Yes, I'm Brittany and you must be..." Her mind suddenly went blank.

"Alex. Alex Crawford, Chad's friend. You called him about a deck?"

As she unlocked the screen, she realized she wasn't quite ready yet to allow a stranger inside, especially a male stranger.

"Yes, I did. It's nice to meet you, Alex. Let's walk around back and I'll show you what I have in mind," she said. She frowned as she realized there was no car in her driveway. "Did you walk here?" she asked.

His eyes were a warm blue that stood out against his tanned face and was complemented by his slightly shaggy dark hair. "I live three doors up." He pointed up the street to the Walker home that had been on the market for a while.

"How long have you lived there?"

"I moved in about six weeks ago," he replied as they

walked around the side of the house.

That explained why she didn't know the Walkers had moved out and Mr. Hard Body had moved in. Six weeks ago she'd still been living at her brother Benjamin's house trying to heal from the trauma she'd lived through.

As they reached the backyard she motioned toward the broken brick patio just outside the back door. "What I'd like is a wooden deck big enough to hold a barbecue pit and an umbrella table and, of course, lots of people."

He nodded and pulled a tape measure from his tool belt. "An outdoor entertainment area," he said.

"Exactly," she replied and watched as he began to walk the site. The last thing Brittany had wanted to think about over the past eight months of her life was men. But looking at Alex Crawford definitely gave her a slight flutter of pure feminine pleasure.

Will Brittany be able to heal in the arms of Alex,
her hotter-than-sin handyman...or will a second
psychopath silence her forever? Find out in
TOOL BELT DEFENDER
Available January 2012
from Harlequin® Romantic Suspense
wherever books are sold.

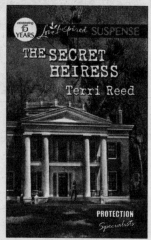

Harlequin®

INTRIGUE

USA TODAY BESTSELLING AUTHOR

DELORES FOSSEN

CONTINUES HER THRILLING MINISERIES

THE LAWMEN OF
SILVER CREEK
Ranch

When the unthinkable happens and children are stolen
from a local day care, old rivals Lieutenant Nate Ryland
and Darcy Burkhart team up to find their kids.
Danger lurks at every turn, but will Nate and Darcy
be able to catch the kidnappers before
the kidnappers catch them?

NATE

Find out this January!

USA TODAY **bestselling author**

Penny Jordan

brings you her newest romance

PASSION
AND THE PRINCE

Prince Marco di Lucchesi can't hide his proud
disdain for fiery English rose Lily Wrightington—
or his attraction to her! While touring the palazzos
of northern Italy, the atmosphere heats up…until
shadows from Lily's past come out….

*Can Marco keep his passion under wraps
enough to protect her, or will it unleash itself, too?*

Find out in January 2012!